THE
DOLL HOUSE
BRIDES

Soleil

S.M. WEBB

DEDICATION

For the romance lovers who dream of whimsical fantasy and the whimsical fantasy lovers who dream of romance: the world is a little better with you in it. Dream on.

Once, when you were in the prime of your life and never looked or felt better, you caught the eye of a thief who had managed to slip through the veils of time. He was drawn to the spark within you and enchanted by your unique features. The thief resolved to capture what he admired most and replicate it in another time, far in the future.

You were alone when he approached, lost in your usual thoughts of this and that and all too susceptible to his spell. In a trick of the light, with a flick of his wrist and the prick of a rose thorn, eight drops of your blood were stolen. When he left, he took your memories of the encounter and all evidence with him.

The thief would think of you often, seeing your resemblance in the faces of the female nymphs he altered with your beauty, a proprietary blend of magic, and other natural wonders: the delicate softness of flowers, the brilliance of gemstones, and the celestial elements of the sky. People around the world were awestruck by the sight of them.

Their physical features, though, were outshone by their spark—*your* spark.

TABLE OF CONTENTS

GOODBYE GIFTS AND IMPLICATIONS

Soleil

The Doll House, Northern Nymph Lands

The Doll House was an homage to all things feminine and charming with scalloped siding, gingerbread trim, and ornamental supports. It was painted and decorated in the same colors inside and out: baby pink and a pale satin cream. Soleil had not expected to return to her childhood home so soon. One of her sisters, Rosette, had sent an urgent letter by hawk that evening. Soleil was curious to know what could not wait for her in-person attendance at the funeral service for their guardian, a mere two days away.

Visiting on such short notice would have been an impossible feat for anyone else in foreign lands, but Soleil and her sisters had a special connection to the Doll House. It was one of the perks of being adopted by a wizard. Ivan

Cherub had adopted three sets of biological twins and ensured each of them could visit the Doll House from anywhere in the world, at any time, in spirit. Tonight, Soleil left her body in the Snow Fae Lands, slumbering alone in a bed meant for two. Marriage, for her, was lonely—but her sisters did not need to know that.

Soleil appeared directly in the parlor. The walls of the oversized gathering place were papered in a design of satin ribbons tied into bows. Two white tufted loveseats and one chaise lounge sat atop the light ash wood floors, and a baby pink grand piano stood off to one side. On the piano were five gift boxes in various sizes, uniformly wrapped in white gold paper with rose gold bows. Soleil considered, then dismissed, the possibility that the gifts were the reason that Rosette had called her here. That could have waited.

Rosette was there in the flesh, as the Doll House was still her primary residence. She stood before the piano in a burgundy dress, her hair fixed in a high ponytail atop her head, and her hands clenched together. There was a solemn tilt to the deep pink lips that matched her hair, eyes, and the sprinkle of freckles across her pale pink nose.

Soleil's twin, Stella, was also physically present, leaning on one elbow in the chaise lounge, her black pants and loose white blouse slightly rumpled. Her long pewter and purple hair was down, a few ringlets framing her silver-skinned face. Stella and Soleil would be identical if not for the tinkering of their wizard guardian. They had the same face and curls and general build, but Stella was magically imbued with the particles of a star stream while Soleil was transformed with the rays of the sun, in gold and bronze.

"You got here quickly," Soleil noted. Stella attended school in the Snow Fae Lands, on the opposite coast from Soleil.

"I left early in the morning." Stella stretched her legs and sat up from the lounge. "You just missed the others. They ghosted in and out." She nodded toward the gift boxes on the piano. "These are goodbye gifts from Cherub. They showed up at each of our bedroom doors. Of course, you can't open yours until you get here in person."

Soleil recounted the packages. There were only five. "Who opened theirs?"

"I did," Rosette said, her tense expression softening as she tugged at the side of her gown's skirt. A fuzzy, hot pink pup looked out from behind her feet. "Don't be shy. This is Soleil."

The pup scampered forward and tilted back its head, letting out a scratchy, underdeveloped howl. Soleil stared at the cub. "He left us pets?"

"Apparently," Stella replied.

"Why didn't you open yours?"

Stella pointed down at Rosette's pet. "Because that's a *wolf,* and I have the largest package. According to the card, they're sleeping and magically sustained until we are ready to open them."

Rosette bent to pat her cub on the head. "And they will never grow up and leave us."

"Does that mean it won't grow at all?" Soleil wondered out loud.

Stella eyed the pink baby wolf suspiciously. "Time will tell."

"She," Rosette clarified, scooping up the little wolf to nestle her in the crook of one arm. "According to the card, they're all female. I haven't decided on a name for her yet."

Soleil imagined her sister would come up with something cute and sweet, but that too, could wait. "Your letter was sent urgently," Soleil reminded her.

Rosette dipped her head. "A representative with the council stopped by to inform us that they have Cherub's last will and testament. I inherited the Doll House, but no one else was named."

There was a slight, involuntary lift to Soleil's shoulder. "That's not so strange." She left it unsaid that Rosette was the only one of them who was neither married nor betrothed because it was a sensitive subject. Rosette wanted to be married, and Cherub promised she would be, but told her he was still working on the right match.

"Well, you see, Cherub's passing prompted the council to look into our adoption records, and, uh . . ." her voice trailed off.

"There aren't any," Stella finished for her, a sparkle in her pewter and purple eyes. "Do you know what that means?"

Soleil's head wobbled in answer, going from a nod to a shake. If there were no adoption records, where did they all come from? All they knew was that Cherub only took in orphaned infant twins. Now that Cherub was gone, they might never know their true origins. He had died two days prior in an accident at sea, and Soleil was still processing that event.

Cherub had been kind to her and her sisters. They attended top schools and never wanted for any material thing. He had arranged favorable betrothals for them with well-off, well-respected families, but Soleil had never felt close to him the way children ought to be close with their parents. She barely knew him.

Stella leaned forward. "If Cherub was not legally our guardian, then he had no right to enter into betrothal contracts on our behalf."

Soleil drew back. "No, I suppose he didn't." The implications whirled through her mind. For the three sisters who had not wed, it was simple enough. Rosette was not betrothed, and the betrothal contracts for the other two were unenforceable. *But what does this mean for those of us who have already married?*

Soleil hadn't realized she'd voiced the question until Stella answered her. "That's up to you."

CHAPTER 1

NYMPHCESS

Soleil

Icelyn, Snow Fae Lands

Princess Soleil Kanamori turned another page, holding the book away from her to present the illustrations to the fae children. "But the humans could not coexist in peace, and so, their world collapsed. Everything they had built dissolved into ash and was swallowed into the earth. Rid of the toxins, the land, sea, and sky were renewed. When the few human and animal survivors breathed in the purified air, their minds were connected by a shared language, and their bodies were transformed by divine magic. A mighty wind blasted them across the globe, sorted by their new magical traits. People who could summon wings and fly became known as the fae—"

"Like us!" a child yelled.

"Yes, fae like you. And people who could wield magic were called nymphs, like me." She murmured a spell, and the open book balanced itself on the tip of her index finger. A hushed *woah* came from the children, and another page turned. "The fae and nymphs forged new cultures, abandoning some of the old human ways while reviving others. Although there is still crime here and there, we share an innate understanding that our leaders must not fall into the ways of hatred and destruction like the humans before us." The book closed and dropped into her lap.

"Why do the dragon fae live far away from everyone else?" a boy mused. "They don't like us?"

Soleil folded her hands atop the book. Everyone knew of the elusive species that could shift into massive beasts, but they kept to the Dragon Fae Islands and declined visitors. "I have never met a dragon fae myself, but just because they keep to their own does not mean they don't like us."

Small hands went up around the room, and she called on a girl with pigtails. "Why do you look like that?"

Soleil was used to this. She had the soft points at the tops of her ears and a female nymph's black lashes that lengthened and curled at the outer edges of her eyes, but many of her features were unnatural to fae and nymphs alike. Golden strands shimmered in her bronze ringlets, and her eyes matched with flecks of gold. Her lips were a bronzed pink and coated in a light gloss, but it was her skin that garnered the most attention. People couldn't help but look for a layer of paint or the seeping stain of a dye, but there was none. Her skin was a permanent, shining gold.

"My sisters and I were adopted by a wizard nymph when we were babies. He transformed each of us with magic that he blended with his favorite things, like the rays of the sun."

One child concentrated on her, then lit up. "Oh, that's you. *You're* the sun."

She winked at him, then called on another child. "My parents call you a *Nymphcess* because you're our princess, but you're also a nymph."

A lump formed in her throat. She would not be their princess for long, but the children did not know that. Soleil forced a smile.

"Where's Prince Kai?" someone else asked.

Her smile slipped as her mind raced to come up with an acceptable response. It hadn't occurred to her that a child would ask this question. Perhaps it should have.

She and the prince had been wed only two weeks ago. His voice had been low and cool as he recited their vows. He slipped a sparkling ring on her finger, pressed cold lips to hers, and their marriage was official. He stayed at the reception just long enough to properly thank everyone for attending. Then, he vanished.

That evening, Soleil had found a single-line letter on the nightstand of the bedchamber they were meant to share:

I will be away on business for an undeterminable amount of time.

Prince Kai

A voice boomed from the back of the room. "Prince Kai has his hands full at present, looking after Icelyn for the Emperor." The children all turned, and Soleil expelled a breath, grateful for her friend's interruption. "Who can name the region on the other side of Kanamori proper, ruled by Prince Wren?"

The kids called out the answer together: "Glacia!"

"Impressive." Vynn Marius tapped a finger to his chin, glancing up. "And which is the *best* region?"

"Icelyn!"

He gave a mock scowl. "No, no. It's Glacia!"

Soleil stifled a giggle as objections mixed with laughter rose from the audience. The teachers stepped in, shepherding the now rambunctious children back to their classrooms. A receiving line led by the schoolmaster and administrative staff bowed and thanked her for the reading, and she, in turn, thanked them for the invitation.

When she made it to the end of the line, Vynn stood waiting with their cloaks draped across his arm. He was dressed casually today, in a cream cable knit sweater over charcoal trousers. His blond hair was brushed back, and a shadow of stubble covered the lower half of his tanned face.

"I was not expecting to see you here."

"I wasn't sure you would be here either," he replied, a sympathetic note to his voice. "I received a letter from Emmie last night."

Although Vynn had been raised in the Snow Fae Lands, he had met and befriended her sister, Emmie, while studying abroad. Soleil had only met him a few months before the wedding, but he checked on her frequently. She suspected Emmie put him up to it.

"How are you?" he prompted, referring to Cherub's passing. She doubted he knew about the Nymph Council's discovery yet, since Emmie too had just learned it the night before.

"I am well enough, considering." They walked together toward the main doors of the school. She side-eyed his face. "Are you growing a beard?"

Vynn rubbed his jaw. "Preparing for squall season."

The Snow Fae Lands were as exquisite as they were dangerous, especially for foreigners whose bodies were not built for the cold. It was never *not* snowing, but from

November to February, squalls blew through each week, coating everything in ice and piling drifts up to the second story. People gathered and stored plenty of supplies so they would not have to leave their homes, but the emperor's soldiers were on patrol as much as possible, looking for anyone who may have been stranded.

"I am leaving for the Nymph Lands tomorrow morning," she told him. The timing with the impending storms could not be better. In a matter of weeks, everyone would be stuck inside. It could be months before the public realized she was gone, depending on how the season went.

Vynn lowered his voice. "It would be my honor to escort you if needed."

Her cheeks burned. Vynn knew as well as she did that the prince hadn't been busy at all. He'd been visiting with his brother Wren in Glacia.

"I should have been more prepared for that question," she admitted. "Their parents will be gossiping soon."

"It's only been two weeks. Most have presumed you were on your honeymoon, and the prince's staff is discreet."

Only two weeks. That was fourteen days of waking up in a massive bed meant for two, alone. It was fourteen days of not knowing what her prince was thinking or whether their marriage was doomed. It would not have occurred to Soleil to give up so soon, though, if not for the annulment option she now had.

"And if he remains at his brother's home for another two weeks?" she asked. Not that it mattered. She was leaving tomorrow.

"Then people will gossip, but only until some new scandal emerges, and it always does."

Vynn should know. His father had been caught in an affair with the empress—Kai's father's first wife. The emperor eventually remarried and had Kai and his brothers with his second wife. It could not have been easy for Vynn to rise above the reputation attached to his family name, but he did, and now he served as Prince Wren's legal advisor. He had persevered, and so could Soleil, if she had any intention of staying.

"This will pass," he promised.

Soleil wished she could warn him that she would not be returning from the Nymph Lands, but did not want to burden him with such a secret. She rolled her shoulders back. "I appreciate the offer of an escort, but I will be fine."

Ever the gentleman, Vynn dropped the matter. He walked her to her carriage and bowed as the footman opened the door. "If you change your mind, or if you need anything at all, I am at your service."

"Thank you, Vynn."

Dapple-gray horses pulled the gleaming silver carriage away from the schoolhouse. Fluffy snowflakes whirled by the window, blurring her view. She would miss these lands and the dreams she once had for her life here. In her mind's eye, she and Prince Kai could have been happy. They would have children—lots of them—with bronzed strands in their dark hair. Some would have wings, and some would wield magic, and each of them would know they were deeply loved. Soleil could no longer entertain those fantasies.

"No matter," she told herself. "I will adjust."

She focused on the next steps. The prince's staff did not yet know of her guardian's passing. Soleil intended to send the necessary letters late this evening by regular courier. She suspected that the head maid, Magda, would want to send them by hawk, as was customary for time-sensitive matters. Soleil would insist that the prince was too busy to be disturbed. She was counting on the maid's loyalty to prevent her from admitting the prince was *not* busy; to do so would be to call him a liar.

The letter to the emperor should be formal with the proper deference to his title. It should be brief, but not so brief as to appear rude. She would not mention the annulment. That could wait until she reached the Nymph Lands.

Soleil did not have to put as much thought into the message to Prince Kai. She knew exactly what that letter should say.

CHAPTER 2

GO HOME, KAI

Kai

Glacia, Snow Fae Lands

If time flew as Kai could, he would be in a deep, dreamless slumber, as far from his troubles as only his unconscious could take him. Instead, time dragged its cruel talons across the barren rock earth of his days, forcing the prince to search for relief elsewhere. It had not escaped his attention that he was becoming insufferable. He didn't even want to be around himself.

Kai turned a page of the history text on the human days, and the book was snatched out of his hands.

"That was unnecessary," Kai grumbled, sitting up in the velvet recliner in his brother's library to glare at him. "Pompous, arrogant—"

Wren interrupted with his own choice words. "Rude, inattentive—"

"Pardon?" He would grant his brother that he'd been sullen of late, but he was never rude or inattentive. His manners were above reproach.

"Rude and inattentive husband," Wren said, sinking into the wing-backed chair opposite of the recliner. He was a little shorter than Kai, but their general build and facial features were strikingly similar. Their father's genes were strong.

Kai sat back. "Ah. That."

"Yes, that. That lovely nymph has gone to great lengths to embrace our customs, win over our people, and run your manor by herself. It's as though she were a born princess with no husband at all."

Kai ground his teeth together. This was not at all how the marriage he hadn't wanted was supposed to go. Soleil was a spoiled rich girl whose doting father arranged for her to become a princess. She was supposed to be competent but not exceptional. Self-absorbed but trained in social niceties. Unfortunately, Magda's regular reports did not support his assumptions.

By all accounts, Soleil was sharp of mind and gentle in spirit. She was vibrant and thoughtful. His anticipation of Magda's next daily letter grew such that he was anxious about it. With each tear of the envelope, he prayed *this* message would justify his absence. Then he would go home and resume his life as prince, separate from hers as princess.

Wren sighed. "You're too old to behave like this."

"Not as old as you," he joked, aware he was only proving his brother's point. "Not ancient like Atamai."

In truth, there were only two years between Kai and his eldest brother and one year between Kai and Wren. Each of them had been conceived in love, but when their parents were of advanced age. After a brutal betrayal and divorce, Kai's father had finally found the one.

Their mother died of natural causes when Kai was just a teen, and their father died of a broken heart shortly thereafter. Before he passed, he expressed his regret over waiting too long to have children and decreed that his sons must be married by the age of twenty-five. If they did not choose their own bride, they would be married to someone their father and the royal advisors had pre-selected. The decree was delivered by the royal advisors on Atamai's twenty-fourth birthday.

Exceedingly clever and not one to bow to convention, Atamai immediately married a widow on her deathbed. Obnoxiously fortunate, Wren had already met the love of his life. And then there was Kai, who was neither especially clever nor fortunate in this instance. He was twenty-two when he learned of his fate and had strenuously protested, beseeching Atamai to find some way to overrule or at least delay their father's decree. Kai had no intention of courting anyone for another twenty-five years; his duty was first to Icelyn, and he and his brothers were still considered young rulers. He promised to marry by fifty and produce an heir by sixty. God willing, he would have a full hundred and forty years with his children.

Alas, the only way out of the betrothal contract was to marry someone he did not love before twenty-five or resign as prince. In the end, Kai's dedication to Icelyn was greater than his disdain for arranged marriage. He went through with his father's choice: Soleil. The marriage would be a sham either way, but at least Kai hadn't participated in selecting a bride for the loveless union. That would have made him as guilty in this scheme as his father and Ivan Cherub.

"It's not as though she is unkind," Wren prodded, "or unpleasant to gaze upon."

That all depended on how one defined unpleasant. Having refused any meeting beforehand, Kai had been thoroughly unprepared for how stunning Soleil was. The first and last time he saw her was at their wedding. Her golden skin was sheathed in white lace, and her glossed lips had vowed to cherish him the rest of their days. It was all he could do to chase the memory from his mind and hold firm to his conviction that no one should be forced to wed.

In the days that followed, he filled his calendar with busywork, reviewing minor issues that had already been handled by trusted nobility. When that didn't work, he shifted course and packed his schedule with his favorite leisure activity: reading. So far, that was not working either.

By contrast, Soleil was reportedly excelling in her new role. She took to her duties as princess with poise and grace and never once complained of his absence. It bothered Kai that the foreign bride he did not want was managing his home well without him. It absolutely killed him to think she was sleeping in his bed, every night, alone. He too often wondered what she wore for nightclothes.

"No one should be forced into marriage," Kai said at last. "I had no intention of looking for a bride for another twenty-five years."

"Yes, you've mentioned that," Wren replied dryly. "Do you want my advice?"

"I do not."

"Get a good night's sleep and wake up early with a strong mug of coffee. Then head home. If you leave at dawn and stick to the high roads through Kanamori proper, you might arrive in time for dinner."

"I'm aware of the distance between our manors by carriage," Kai drawled. "You don't want me here?"

Wren tossed his words back at him. "I do not."

"Hm. Baylee will miss me."

His brother's mouth tilted upward. "My wife may find your sullenness charming, but she is the only one. Your sour mood is scaring my staff and annoying me. More importantly, I have a duty to my sister-in-law and have indulged you for too long." He pitched forward. "*Go home*, Kai."

A knock came from the inside of the entryway. The brothers stood as Baylee glided into the library. She was a dainty thing for a fae, with curly black hair, dark skin, and deep brown eyes. She dressed her slight form in a regal silken gown. The embroidery at the dropped waistline cradled the small bump of early pregnancy. "I'm afraid I must interrupt."

Wren's eyes gleamed at the sight of his wife. "You are never an interruption, darling. What is it?"

Baylee paced forward with an envelope in her hand. "A letter just arrived."

Kai rolled his eyes to the ceiling. "If it's another long-winded missive from Vynn Marius, toss it in the fire, and find a new advisor—one whose father didn't have an affair with our father's first wife."

"Vynn is an excellent advisor and not responsible for his father's betrayal. I know he was a twit as a kid, but that was a long time ago."

As a teen, Kai had learned firsthand that Vynn wasn't much better than the male who had spawned him. In college, though, Vynn had turned his back on his father. Even after he'd been cut off financially, the young lord was not swayed. Maybe Wren was right, and he had changed. Maybe he hadn't. Kai didn't care.

Baylee pivoted toward Kai. "This letter is for you, from your wife. It just arrived by hawk."

"By hawk?" Kai turned the envelope over in his hands. "It isn't marked urgent."

"I thought that was strange, too. Whatever it is, it must have just happened. She was at a school this morning, reading to the children."

Kai broke the wax seal that had been stamped with the Kanamori imperial crest. "Keeping tabs on my bride?"

She crinkled her nose at him. "Someone has to. I would very much like to see my sister-in-law again, Kai. We barely spoke at the wedding." She had told him this often since he had arrived. Each time, Kai offered some quip about Baylee being too adorable to act like such a nag, and she would tease him about being too educated to be so obstinate. The lighthearted jabs would end in a laugh, but Kai could not manage any humor now.

His jaw clenched as he re-read the note from his wife:

I am returning home for an undeterminable amount of time.

Princess Soleil

The audacity set him back. Did she think she could abandon her role as princess? Abandon their marriage after only a couple of weeks? She had the nerve to send him a message that she was leaving *like this?* An angry flush burned his face as the blood rushed to his head, drowning out more reasonable considerations, like the fact that he had abandoned her first. He had even given her the words for the letter he was crumbling in his hands.

Kai swore a curse under his breath and turned on his heel, striding out of his brother's library and heading straight for his carriage.

CHAPTER 3

AN UNEXPECTED ESCORT

Soleil

Icelyn, Snow Fae Lands

Long ago, Soleil had resolved to make peace with the things she could not change, but Cherub's death and her impending annulment underscored everything she did like dark threads stitched into each thought and menial task. It was all she could think about as she packed. She ran a finger over the clusters of blue and white diamonds that encircled her wedding band and matched the tiara she wore at public events. She would leave the tiara behind for the trip home and had considered leaving the wedding band as well, but the staff would notice. Soleil wanted to wait a few days after the service before alerting anyone that she would not be returning.

She took in the decadent bed chamber one last time. The bed was covered in silver and cobalt blue blankets made of rich velvet. Thick, intricately woven rugs warmed the floors. Veins of blue and silver swirled in the white marble underfoot and around the fireplace. An oversized chair sat beside a round pedestal table across from the hearth.

A private balcony overlooked the rolling snow-covered hills and a sliver of the frigid ocean beyond. When the snowfall was light, she would stand at the glass doors and watch penguins frolic with snow seals among the icebergs. She turned away with a heavy heart and closed the bedroom door behind her.

No matter, she reminded herself, *I will adjust.*

On her way out, the head maid fussed over Soleil's old cloak. The rose gold garment was made of brushed satin and lightly lined with fleece. Magda worried it was not warm enough to brave the Snow Fae Lands. It wasn't, but the trip to the docks was not far and the carriage was warm. More importantly, it was sentimental. It reminded Soleil of her hometown, Bloom.

The docks along the shore of Icelyn were not far from the manor. Soleil's trip was quiet and uneventful. When the carriage rolled to a stop, the door opened. She scooted forward and her mouth fell open as she craned her head back to look up.

Prince Kai appeared as sharp and as cold as she remembered from their wedding day. Sparkling snowflakes caught in his black locks, his bangs falling to the edges of his dark eyes. Beneath his heavy, fur-lined cloak, he dressed his tall and leanly muscled frame in a deep blue tailored suit with his silver cravat undone, dangling around his collar.

"Leaving so soon, princess?"

It took a moment for Soleil to realize she was gawking at him. Closing her mouth, she scooted back as he climbed inside. "I . . . you received my letter?"

"I did." He flashed a smile. "Late last night."

Last night? By regular courier, he should not have received it until this morning. Magda must have sent her note by hawk, against her wishes.

His expression was assessing and detached at the same time, as if he were reviewing the details of a problem he had already solved. "Are you feeling ill?"

She frowned. "No."

"No? Not at all feverish? Because in your letter, you appeared confused. Unless I am mistaken, *home* is the manor you just left."

The comment caught her off guard. She hadn't thought he would care about the letter at all, but she had no regrets. Writing it had been therapeutic for her. "My childhood home," she corrected briskly, "Cherub's estate."

"Ah. I confess I do not know how these matters are handled in nymph culture, but here, it is customary to await your spouse's acknowledgment before taking leave of your responsibilities."

Soleil wasn't sure which she found most insulting, that he had the gall to refer to himself as her spouse, or the way her heart skipped a beat to hear him acknowledge it. She lifted her chin. "In nymph culture, one makes exceptions when there is an untimely death." She felt no small amount of triumph when surprise flashed in his eyes. "Cherub died in an accident at sea."

"I . . ." he began with a small shake to his head. "I am sorry for your loss."

She gave a curt nod. "I really must be on my way. My sisters are expecting me."

He studied her again, then exited the carriage, offering her a hand. She accepted, stepping out to find a matching royal carriage parked beside hers. Last she'd heard, he was staying at Wren's manor. The royal carriages were faster than civilian transport, but it would have taken him all night to travel by carriage to the docks to intercept her. Had her letter bothered him that much? Or had the hawk found him on his way home?

The wind whipped around them, and Soleil shivered. Icy air rushed through the thin material of her cloak and lifted the hood from her head.

Kai's brows knitted together, and he tugged her hood back into place. "Do you not have a suitable cloak?"

"This one is customary for the Northern Nymph Lands."

He shrugged out of his cloak and draped it over her shoulders. The oversized garment was warm from his body heat. It swallowed her form, shielding her from the wind. "Then you can change when we get there," he grumbled.

She stammered a moment. "We?"

"I've no intention of letting my wife travel overseas unescorted." He moved around her to meet the footmen at the back of the carriages.

Soleil watched him go, dumbstruck. This would not do at all. She could not leave him if he was coming with her. Even if she hadn't intended to leave him, his actions were presumptuous, showing up here like he hadn't left *her* on their wedding night and embarrassed her with his absence. She ought to be infuriated, but all she could muster was minor annoyance overwhelmed by curiosity.

CHAPTER 4

A SUNBURST IN WINTERLAND

Kai

Icelyn, Snow Fae Lands

Romanticizing a memory was the folly of poets, musicians, and other artists who skated along the fringe of reality. Kai was more grounded than that. Since their wedding, visions of Soleil plagued him at all hours of the day and night in vivid details that he thought must be inflated. Much to his dismay, she was more beautiful than he remembered.

She had attended school with the Snow Fae for years but still looked like a stranger in a strange land. The dark blue velvet interior of the royal carriage was a cool contrast to her gold skin and the bronze ringlets that she had pinned into a bun. Even now, practically drowning in the weight of his cloak, Soleil's loveliness could not be dimmed. She was a sunburst in Winterland.

Beauty, no matter how striking, was not as important to Kai as merit, so he set that aside, contemplating her demeanor instead. It was shocking and sad to learn of anyone's accidental death, but she did not appear all that upset over her father's loss. The fae and nymphs were hearty people; their skin and bones did not break easily. They occasionally fell ill, but the illness was rarely terminal. Most people lived a full two hundred years before crossing into the afterlife. How could someone not grieve the untimely death of their parent?

"Prince and Princess Kanamori." A feminine voice caught his attention. "It is my honor to provide your expedited passage to the Northern Nymph Lands."

The captain appeared beyond the footmen, dressed in a burnished gold uniform and cap. Just beyond her, a sky scamp perched on six short legs. Evolved from domestic puppies of the human days, the sky scamps were cute creatures, with short snouts and soft, floppy ears. This one was black and brown, fresh snow glistening in its dense fur coat. They were exceptionally strong. Half the size of a royal ship, their narrow, serpent-like bodies could tow multiple cargo loads at a time but attached to this scamp's tale was a carriage in Sun Fae colors.

Kai glanced down at Soleil. "You're not taking the royal ship?"

"My sister Phire arranged for transport."

Ah, Prince Gage's wife. He knew Gage already; the Snow Fae and Sun Fae royalty often hosted each other. Kai had missed their wedding, but at his, Phire had been at Gage's side, each of them glowing like a couple in love.

He remembered the rest of Soleil's sisters from their wedding, too. It had been disconcerting to see them all together and not because of their colors. Their faces were so similar that all six females presented as biological sisters, but only the twins were technically related.

The footman remained still, waiting for Kai's approval before moving the luggage. He eyed the animal again. Sky scamps came in and out of port pulling carts for trade but were not typically used by the Snow Fae for personal travel. It wasn't unheard of, but it was considered more dignified for royals and nobles to travel between continents by sea. The ships were nearly as fast as a scamp. When neither were fast enough, the fae would fly. If Kai had missed Soleil's carriage, he would have found her in the skies.

He could fly Soleil to the Nymph Lands himself in half the time if he thought her nymph body could withstand the cold of these skies. Kai immediately chastised the thought for the image it evoked. Soleil in his arms and clinging to him was an idea that would lead to other visions best not entertained if he was committed to his moral objections—and he was.

Soleil seemed to read the hesitation on his face. "I know it is not customary here, but it has already been arranged by my sister."

The sky scamp gave a snort as if in agreement. It wasn't unreasonable. The carriage was a royal one, even if it wasn't his own. He paced forward, inspecting the hitch at the beast's tail. It looked sturdy enough.

More importantly, Kai was too exhausted to protest. He had intended to sleep during his trip home, but had spent most of the night before fuming over Soleil's message. "All right."

Wings coated in sand-colored feathers sprang from the captain's back. She glided upward, patting the beast's head before landing in the saddle. The footman fetched their luggage, and Kai guided Soleil with a hand at her elbow, walking her to the transport and helping her in. He paused to cover a yawn before settling across from her.

Inside, the seats were upholstered in a tan damask fabric with subtle, bronze designs. As they took flight, Soleil leaned toward the window, and Kai let the heavy lids of his eyes drift closed. His last thought before succumbing to sleep was how annoying it was that the Sun Fae's royal colors complemented his wife better than his own.

CHAPTER 5

CHILDISH CRUSH

Soleil
Somewhere in the Skies

Her husband snored. It wasn't at all loud or jarring—just a soft snuffle in and a low sigh out. She wasn't sure if it was because he was sitting up as he slept or if he always snored, but it was almost endearing. The steady rhythm was conducive to the meditative state required for slipping away from her physical form. Soleil left her snoozing husband along with her body and entered the Doll House, ghosting down the halls to look for Stella. It was midafternoon there, and Soleil knew her twin would be in one of two places: in the conservatory, indulging a sweet treat or tending to her garden by hand.

Soleil paused in the conservatory, taking note of the plants and floral arrangements that had been crowded there, then exited the home. Stella's garden lay on one side of the house. It was a lush expanse of flowering vines, creeping clover, and silvery sprigs of aromatic herbs bordered by wooden beams that had been spelled to keep the garden thriving year-round.

Working in the dirt was unnecessary. Everything Stella did with her hands could be done with a spell, but she enjoyed the work. Once the herbs were ready to harvest, she'd toil away in the kitchen, formulating teas for every season, mood, and malady.

Stella looked up from where she knelt on the ground, and Soleil noted the mass of tangled curls about her shoulders. Neatness was often an afterthought for her twin. "Prince Kai and I won't be here for another couple of hours. You'll have time to freshen up."

Stella's eyes drifted sideways, following her sister's line of sight to her hair, then snapped back to Soleil. "He's coming?"

"Of course. Why wouldn't he?" Soleil replied smoothly. She had not told her sisters that she'd be returning alone and now that she wouldn't be, there was no reason to address it.

Stella pulled off her gardening gloves as she stood. "I know about him taking off after the wedding. Emmie told me. She heard it from Vynn."

Soleil resisted a groan in response. Vynn and Emmie were good friends. She should have considered he would mention it. "Do the others know?"

"I don't think so. Does he know about your annulment option?"

"He does not, and I would prefer to keep it that way, for now."

Stella's lips puckered in a sign of disapproval that she opted not to voice. "What made him decide to come with you?"

"Etiquette, probably, but I need more time with him to know for sure. We haven't gotten to know each other yet."

The prince had declined to meet with her before the wedding. It wasn't like that for her other married sisters. Even her unmarried sisters corresponded with their intended. That was more than Soleil had managed to get from Kai, unless she counted the note he had left on the nightstand.

What little she got from him was confusing at best. His sympathy was sincere, but there was an underlying edge there. He acted as though he were suspicious of her, and Soleil had no idea why. It was an odd thing to be rejected by a stranger. She wished she didn't care at all, but alas, she had come to care for Kai years ago. "I let myself develop a childish crush on him from afar."

Stella already knew this. "Ever since that speech."

Soleil had always known she would be wed to someone in the Snow Fae Lands. When she turned eighteen, Cherub revealed her betrothed would be Prince Kai unless he chose someone else before they turned twenty-five. Cherub had promised to find her another match within the Snow Fae Lands if the prince chose someone else.

Soleil understood why she could not be formally introduced to him when she learned of their betrothal. For one thing, their marriage was not guaranteed. The timing also wasn't ideal. The prince's father had passed the year before, making his eldest brother Atamai the new emperor while dividing the outer territories between Prince Kai and his other brother, Wren. Still, she was curious to catch a glimpse of him in person.

She had dragged Stella to the Winter's End Fair—a royal event where she could see the prince from the crowd. The sight of him made her heart beat a little faster. When the emperor called upon him to make an unplanned speech, he rose to the challenge gracefully.

There was a passion in his voice when he spoke of his people, and Soleil had left the fair inspired. Although she had known their marriage might not go through, she was determined to be worthy of him and the people he served. She had returned to school with a renewed dedication, learning everything she could about the prince, Icelyn, and life in the Kanamori Empire. The more she learned, the more certain she felt that Icelyn was where she was meant to be. Until their wedding day.

"You know he treats his staff and his citizens well," Stella said. "That's not nothing. Did he give you a reason for leaving?"

"Not an honest one. I was beginning to think our marriage might be in name only, like Daisy's."

"Daisy and Jameson talk," Stella pointed out. "Have you told him how you feel?"

"After he's practically rejected me? No, I'm not a glutton for punishment." It would be foolish to make too much of his few thoughtful gestures, but hasty to dismiss them outright. "I need to be sure he's here out of something more than obligation," she decided out loud. "If he isn't, then I'll stay in the Nymph Lands and send him home on his own." That settled, she changed the subject. "Who else is here?"

"Just me and Rosette. Daisy was here to open her gift and get the annulment document from the council's office. Then she left."

Daisy was always zipping around, never staying in one place for too long. She lived in the Northern Nymph Lands, but far from Bloom, on the east coast. "She's going through with the annulment?"

"It's already done. The council says the annulment is unilateral, so the husband doesn't have to sign, but

Jameson wouldn't contest it anyway. If you want yours, you'll have to get it from the council and sign with one of their staff as a witness."

"And if I do nothing, I stay married." It was a simple enough process. If only the decision were that easy. "What are you and Emmie going to do about your betrothals?"

"There's nothing to do; they're void. Emmie is going back to the Sun Fae Lands to tell her would've-been groom in person, after the service. She says if he still wants to go through with the marriage, she will."

That sounded about right. Emmie had always been practical and thought of her match as a good fit.

"I have a message ready to go back with the crow-hawk, and I can't wait to shove it in his obnoxious beak."

Stella's betrothal was arranged over the summer, just when she had grown comfortable with the idea of never being betrothed. The arrangement was odd from the start. Cherub would not share any details about her intended—not his surname, where exactly he resided, or what he did for a living. All they knew was that he went by Nik, and his details were confidential prior to the wedding. They assumed he was somewhere in the Snow Fae Lands since that was where Cherub had sent Stella to school, although on the opposite coast from Soleil, in Frahst.

His letters were sent by a distinctly all black hawk with no return address. The messages were sweet and kind but told her nothing. Rosette thought it was romantic, but Stella had been perpetually annoyed since the first letter.

"I think your ire might be misdirected at a bird."

"That bird is a menace! Squawking at my window before dawn, swooping at my head to deliver letters. It follows me on my trips to the islands." Although the Snow Fae Lands were far from barren, the weather made them challenging to explore. The outer islands of Frahst were densely forested, had a milder climate, and were a quick trip from Stella's campus.

"Last month, it found me at a sidewalk café and took off with my apple tart!" She huffed. "I was *starving* until brunch."

Soleil held back a giggle. Stella ate five times a day: breakfast, brunch, lunch, teatime, and dinner. "Will you return to Frahst?"

"Yeah. All my stuff is there, and my rent and tuition are paid through spring. I don't like the idea of Rosette being here alone, but she insists she'll be fine."

"How is she doing?" Once the words were out, Soleil realized she didn't have to ask. Rosette loved Cherub. To her mind, he could do no wrong. When he arranged Stella's marriage before hers—knowing Stella did not want to be married but Rosette did—she maintained that he must have had good reasons while having no idea what those reasons were.

"She's sad and a little anxious, I think. Baking a lot, which is great for me, but it's going to take time. I'll make her some stronger teas before I go," she said, gesturing with a hand to her herb garden, "and make sure she knows how to make her own in case she needs more. She's looking forward to everyone being home for the service. We'll lift her spirits."

"We will," Soleil agreed. "You said Daisy opened her gift while she was here?"

Stella nodded. "Hummingbird. It follows her everywhere, just like Rosette's wolf, and they have names now. The wolf is Lady Thorn, and the bird is Whim."

"Cute. Did you open yours?"

"Not yet." She lifted her hands in the air in a defensive gesture. "I'll open it when you open yours."

CHAPTER 6

WORLD MOURNING

Kai

Northern Nymph Lands, West Coast

The scent of snow-glazed pine and winterberries clung to his wife's skin and wafted through the carriage, sneaking into Kai's nonsensical dreams of sunbathing in the dead of winter. He awoke to find Soleil staring out the window. Scrubbing a hand over his face, he grumbled under his breath. "Is there anything to see but clouds?"

"Clouds and sea, although we're nearing land now." She faced him. "I don't get to see them from this vantage point as often as the fae do."

The comment prompted another vision of Soleil in his arms in the clouds. It might be doable in the skies over the Northern Nymph Lands. In his cloak, in his arms, she would be warm enough. His gaze snagged on her lips, and she cocked her head to one side. "What?"

Kai lifted his eyes to hers, shoving those thoughts to the dark recesses of his mind where they belonged. He sifted through the facts he had learned about Soleil in the days leading up to their wedding. She studied in the Snow Fae Lands for most of her life, but outside of the Kanamori Empire, in a neighboring region. "You attended college in Snoelle, correct? Princess Baylee is from there."

"While I was there, she was studying in Glacia, where she met your brother."

Yes, he thought, *Wren chose to wed.* Out loud, he asked, "What did you study?"

"Aside from general academics, I studied politics and diplomacy."

"Seems appropriate for an aspiring princess."

"It translates well," she agreed. "As a child, I wanted to be an elected member of the local nymph council or a schoolteacher."

That was unexpected. Serving on the nymph council was akin to royalty, sort of, but being a schoolteacher was a humbling and noble profession, one Kai valued highly. Was she being earnest? Or was this the type of thing she had been coached to say in school or by Cherub?

"Perhaps I'll abdicate my throne and become a scientist or historian. Then you could pursue teaching." It was a bold-faced lie. As much as he enjoyed studying science and history, he would never abandon his people.

If Soleil had any discomfort with the idea, she hid it well. She watched him patiently as if waiting for him to say more. "You must have enjoyed your time reading to children yesterday."

Her expression lifted. "I did. I love children, and it was a welcome distraction from the news."

"From the . . .?" The words stalled in his throat. "You went to the school *after* you learned of your father's death?"

She smoothed her hands atop her lap. "I had already committed and could not leave for the Nymph Lands until today."

The carriage dipped, prompting them to look out the window. They were well into the mountains. He knew the sea lay just behind the ridge, but he could not see it anymore. A pink and white Victorian-style home was nestled amid towering trees. The large plot boasted expansive gardens and a stable. A speckled brick wall surrounded the property, covered in climbing roses with fresh blooms that should have withered away with autumn. A carriage that matched the house was parked in the semi-circle driveway.

Kai wasn't surprised by the size of the estate. He'd only met Cherub briefly, but knew his magic was applauded by high society everywhere. It was said that for the right price, the wizard nymph could create domestic pets from the young of a wild animal and grow full, lush gardens from a few leaves and flower petals.

Soleil inclined her head toward the home. "We call it the Doll House."

Fitting. The carriage door swung open without the aid of a footman, and Kai recalled that the Nymph Lands ran entirely on spells. There was no need for maids, butlers, or footmen here. Nymphs could summon hawks and direct carriages to drive without horses all by uttering a simple spell. They couldn't make anything fly, though. It was generally accepted that the nymphs could not cause a thing or a person to fly any more than the fae could cast a spell.

He stepped out of the carriage and offered Soleil a hand, looking around. A mountain range bordered the meadow where they had landed. Soleil called to the captain, confirming the bags had been magically moved to the house. When the sky scamp departed, Kai took his cloak from Soleil. The late October air was crisp, but the sun was warm.

As they neared the home's entrance, they happened upon Soleil's pink sister, a large bundle of lilies in her arms. "Soleil!"

Kai was reminded of how tall Soleil and her twin were compared to other female nymphs. He could scarcely see Rosette behind the flowers. Her petite figure was clad in a blue eyelet sundress. Her dark pink waves were pulled into a high ponytail, the tresses falling past her lighter, petal pink shoulders. A puppy a half shade brighter than her hair followed, hiding behind her skirt when she stopped before them.

"I'm sure you remember Rosette from our wedding?"

"I do." He made a slight bow. "May I assist?"

Rosette handed over the bouquet. "Thank you. Couriers have been showing up day and night with flowers. The conservatory and patio are full, so we're putting new deliveries in the parlor." There was a sad tilt to her lips. "The world is in mourning."

All but my wife, Kai thought.

Soleil's twin emerged from the house. She dressed in black pants and a loose-fitting lavender blouse. Her hair was damp, as though she had just washed it, the thick pewter and purple ringlets falling to the middle of her back. He wondered if Soleil's hair was that long. It was pinned up every time he'd seen her.

Soleil shared a hug with each sister. Stella offered Kai a smile. "Prince Kai."

He dipped his head. "Hello, Stella."

"Phire and Gage will be here first thing in the morning," Rosette told them, "Emmie should arrive by mid-morning, and Daisy promised to be here on time for the service."

From over Rosette's shoulder, Stella gave an emphatic shake of her head as if to tell them Daisy would *not* be on time. He suppressed a smile. "Where will the service be held?"

"Here," Soleil answered. "Cherub always wanted a small, private service in the garden where he will be planted."

That seemed odd for someone who lived so publicly. He didn't voice the thought, but Stella seemed to pick up on it. "Cherub prided himself on being full of surprises. Speaking of," she added to Soleil, "are you ready to meet your new pet?"

"Pet?" Kai echoed as the nymphs moved on without him.

No one answered. They continued to the entrance, the pink puppy keeping up with Rosette. As he followed with the oversized bouquet of lilies, Kai pondered why they referred to Ivan as *Cherub* rather than father, how they each felt about him, and why he wanted to know.

CHAPTER 7

PRETTY GIRL

Soleil

The theme of the Doll House was consistent from the outside in, feminine and lovely. Pink painted halls and ornamental archways conjured images of the fluffy bathrobes with matching bunny slippers she and her sisters wore as children. Soleil had long ago accepted she could not live here forever, but it would always be special to her and her sisters. She sighed to herself, glad that the house would stay with Rosette.

"What?" Kai prompted from behind her.

Soleil glanced up, encouraged that he noticed her sigh, hopeful that his inquiry was more than politeness. He had slept through most of their trip, which made her think he had not slept, or had not slept well, since receiving her letter. When he was awake, his eyes scarcely left her.

His comment about resigning as prince was absurd. He loved Icelyn too much to walk away. So, he was fishing—trying to ascertain if she only cared about being a princess. *Interesting.*

Instead of answering him, she paused at the bottom of the grand staircase. "Cherub's room and study are on the main floor. Our bedrooms are upstairs, four rooms to the right and four to the left. Two are guest bedrooms."

"Did you have many guests?"

Rosette answered him. "Cherub hosted a lot of dinner parties, but no one stayed overnight."

"He'd intended to transform another set of twins but never did," Stella explained, "so those rooms became guestrooms."

They continued to the foyer, which was indeed filled with floral arrangements from all over the world. No flat surface was open on the coffee table or window ledges. Plants and flowers lined each wall on the floor. There were a few flowers crowded beside the remaining goodbye gifts from Cherub atop the piano as well.

Kai carried the flowers he'd taken from Rosette into the room and deposited them in the far corner. "You weren't exaggerating."

Rosette picked up her wolf pup and cradled her in her arms. "Go on, open your gift," she directed Soleil. "Lady Thorn needs a friend to play with."

The prince frowned, his gaze shifting from Rosette's pet up to the presents. Soleil found her gift amid the others on the piano. It was a mid-sized box that might fit Lady Thorn—not as big as the present addressed to Stella. She crouched to the floor, slipped the ribbon off and lifted the lid.

A tiny gold fox with a white-gold belly swished its full tail as it peered up at her with cinnamon eyes edged by long, dark gold lashes.

"Aren't you a pretty girl." Soleil reached out to pet her head. The kit nodded as though she understood and agreed, then nuzzled into Soleil's hand, her tail curling around her dainty paws.

Rosette set Lady Thorn loose. "Go say hello." The pup obeyed, and each pet sniffed around the other. Lady Thorn's tail began to wag. She scampered to the coffee table, and the fox gave chase. After a few laps, they shifted course, the pup chasing the kit.

Soleil looked pointedly at Stella and her twin heaved a sigh, moving to the piano. She wrapped both arms around her present and set it on the floor. With one tug at the bow, the front panel of the box opened, and her pet rolled out, holding onto its toes. The lilac and light silver animal sprawled at Stella's feet, gazing up at her with purple eyes.

Stella kept her face neutral, but Soleil guessed she was delighted. She loved pandas. Stella bent forward. "How am I supposed to lug you around?"

It was a fair question. The panda was just a cub, but three times the size of Soleil's fox. She could easily lift the ball of fluff into her arms but would tire of carrying it before long.

"Surely, she can walk," Soleil said, although she wasn't sure. It was the shape of a ball, with short, chubby legs.

Lady Thorn and the fox came forward to greet the new pet. The fox nudged the panda in the belly with her snout, and the panda rolled back and then forward two full rotations before planting her paws before her. Lady Thorn let out a happy yip.

"Well, she can roll," Rosette noted.

Kai's brows threaded together as he regarded the last two gifts on the piano. "There are animals in these boxes?"

"Don't worry," Soleil assured him, "they are sleeping and magically sustained in there."

"How?"

"Cherub didn't always share the 'how' of his magic with us," Stella answered, watching her panda, "and he never left any clues either. Every time he left town, he took all his journals with him." She waved a hand toward the piano. "The last two gifts are for the jewels—Phire and Mean Green."

"Don't call her that," Rosette said under her breath to Stella before elaborating for Kai. "She means Emmie. Emmie's just . . . harder to get to know. Don't be offended if she doesn't say much to you." Her dark pink eyes darted to the ceiling as if entertaining an afterthought, then back to him. "And don't be offended if she does."

Kai arched a brow at Soleil, but she had nothing to add. If things were going well between them when Emmie arrived, and she hoped they would be, she would intervene. If they weren't, she'd let Emmie have at him. He did leave her on their wedding night, after all.

Rosette brought the subject back to the new pets. "What are you going to name them?"

Soleil considered her golden kit. "Blaze."

"Yes!" Rosette beamed. "Blaze is perfect!"

"Pudge," Stella declared.

As quickly as it had lit up, Rosette's expression fell. "You can't name her Pudge. It's unkind. She should have a more respectable name. Something sweet or regal."

"All right . . ." Stella pursed her lips as she watched the little panda bumble after the other pets. "Princess Pudge."

Soleil shook her head and Rosette side-eyed Stella before waving her hands in a shooing motion to corral the tiny animals toward the doorway. "We should get started on dinner."

"I'll help," Soleil offered.

"No, Rosette and I can handle it," Stella replied. "Why don't you show Prince Kai about the grounds while there's still some daylight left?"

CHAPTER 8

ACCOMPLISHMENTS

Kai

Perhaps Kai had been possessed by the wayward spirit of an ancestor who delighted in tormenting him the way his brothers did. That seemed the only reasonable explanation for why he was behaving like someone who didn't mind being married. The moment Stella suggested it, he found himself looking forward to being alone with Soleil again.

She allowed him to help her into her cloak and led him through a back door onto a patio that was also crowded with flowers. Most were foreign to him, but he spotted a few from the Snow Fae Lands already. Soon, he expected there would be more glittering winter roses from his people of Icelyn. Atamai would send snowbells that were native to Kanamori proper, and Wren and Baylee would no doubt send the rare ice puffs that were found only in Glacia.

Kai followed Soleil onto a path made of crushed pink crystals. The muted light of the descending sun highlighted her face. Except for the occasional chirp of small animals, the forested grounds were quiet.

They came to a fork in the trail. Soleil took the stepping stones through a circle of wildflowers. At the center sat a bench that was built to ring the base of a large tree, with seats facing outward. There was no tree yet, but a shallow hole had been dug within the ring.

"This is where Cherub will be planted, tomorrow."

It wasn't unusual that Cherub had designated a space to be planted when he died. Lots of people did that. No one lived in their mortal body forever. Trees of loved ones who had passed away sprouted within a year of their remains being planted. Kai imagined that Cherub's tree would grow faster. It might be full-grown within weeks.

It was still odd to him that someone like Cherub wanted a small service. "Will any other family attend?"

"No. He had no living family."

"You mean, except for you and your sisters." She said nothing to that. They doubled back to the main path and moved up toward the stables.

"Do you know anything about your birth families?"

Soleil was slow to answer. "Cherub told us that he only adopted infant twins who had no living parents. That way, we wouldn't know any family but him and each other and he didn't have to worry about the parents wanting us back after he transformed us. He liked things tidy and uncomplicated like that."

"It's a wonder he found so many of you to fit that criteria." She hummed in agreement. "You and Stella are much taller than other female nymphs."

"Only Rosette and Daisy are truly nymph-sized. Magic comes a little easier to them as well. They don't have to concentrate on a spell as much as the rest of us do. Emmie's theory is that we have some fae in our bloodlines."

Kai had to agree. The mention of Emmie made his lips quirk, thinking back to what Stella and Rosette had said. "Rosette seems concerned about my meeting Emmie."

Soleil's grin was luminous in the dwindling light of the evening. "Don't worry. I won't leave you on your own with Emmie."

He couldn't help but chuckle at the unnecessary warning. If anything, he was intrigued.

They came to a stop before the stables. There were no signs of life. "Where are the animals?"

"Cherub sold them as soon as he transformed them into pets. They were never here for long."

Much like his daughters, Kai thought, transformed as infants and then arranged to be married away after college.

"Does it bother you that he altered your appearance as an infant?"

"No," she said simply. "Cherub made us feel special. Stella is my twin, but all of us were connected by the transformation. We've always been close."

"Were you close with Cherub?"

"No one was." Soleil turned from the stables.

He followed for a few steps before he guessed out loud, "You didn't like him."

There was nothing but the sound of their boots atop the gravel path. The sun had dipped behind the purple mountain range, tracing each jagged peak in orange and casting a warm glow on their surroundings. Her expression was obscured in the waning light of evening, but she appeared more lost in recall than sad. When she spoke again, her eyes were on the house. "I did like him. When we were little, I remember thinking he was so proud of us, but . . ." Her gaze drifted from the house to the ground as she seemed to search for the right words. "He traveled a lot, and when he was home, he spent most of his time in his study. We were raised by in-home tutors until we were about twelve, when we were old enough to be unsupervised. For college, he sent us to different regions where he thought we should marry. Only the florals—Rosette and Daisy—stayed in the Doll House, attending a local school just outside of Bloom."

"The florals," he mused aloud. "Are they betrothed to nymphs, then?"

"Daisy married a nymph about a month before our wedding and moved to the east coast. Rosette was never betrothed, although she wanted to be. Cherub swore he was working on a match for her so she could stay in this area. He wanted us to start families all over the world, each twin living on the opposite coast of the same lands. He originally intended to have a pair of twins in the Southern Nymph Lands, too."

Right, Kai thought, recalling that Cherub had wanted to adopt and transform another set of twins but never did.

"He treated us well, and I do believe he was proud of us in his own way, but he did not think of himself as our father." Her gaze lifted to the sky. "We were his accomplishments, not his children."

Kai sucked in a breath, not at all liking how his perspective was rapidly shifting. Soleil was supposed to be a spoiled girl with a simple mind and simple past. She was supposed to be someone he could easily and rightfully avoid, even in marriage. His traitorous mind refused to obey those basic commands anymore.

"What about you?" she asked as they neared the end of the path. "Were you close with your parents before they passed?"

It was a reasonable question, especially since she had told him how she felt about Cherub, but did he want to share this with her? That was the kind of thing happily married couples did, and Kai had been married against his will. So had she.

He stopped walking, and Soleil stopped beside him. "Doesn't it bother you that Cherub arranged marriages for you and your sisters?"

"Not really, no. Arranged marriages aren't uncommon. Some people are married off at eighteen and to someone much older, but Cherub's terms for our engagements were favorable." She brought her hands before her, counting along her fingers. "We would have a higher education and not be married before age twenty-five. Our intended must be within four years of our age, educated, well off, and come from a reputable family." Soleil dropped her hands, her voice softening. "Do you ask because you do not wish to be married to me?"

"I'm opposed to arranged marriages altogether," he corrected. "I didn't wish to be married to anyone." A bitter aftertaste flowed from the words, weighing heavily on his tongue. His conviction wasn't as strong as it was before he found her at the docks. Even if it were, he had no desire to hurt Soleil. It would have been convenient for Kai to write her off as a co-conspirator along with his father and Cherub, but she wasn't. Their marriage was not her fault.

Soleil didn't look hurt, though. She gave a singular nod. "I see."

Stella chose that moment to call to them from the Doll House. "Dinner!"

CHAPTER 9

SLEEPING ARRANGEMENTS

Soleil

If there was any relief to be found in confirming what one already suspected, it was quickly overcome by Soleil's contemplations of what to do next. Her prince was wavering in his objection to their marriage. It was clear in his eyes and clearer still in his voice. His choice of words was also telling. *I didn't want to be married to anyone* was different from *I don't want to be married to anyone*. There was hope for them, then, and Soleil did not want to give up on her dreams of a happy marriage with Kai while there was still hope.

A less pleasant thought niggled at the back of her brain. Kai might be waffling in his feelings about their arranged marriage, but he was also unaware that an annulment was possible. She should tell him, of course. It would be irresponsible not to. She *would* tell him, she told herself. Just not yet.

Soleil led Kai to the dining room, where white walls were capped by a domed ceiling and a candle chandelier made of pink teardrop crystals hung above the round, polished wood table for twelve. He pulled out her chair and then sat beside her. Her sisters exchanged pleasantries with him as they ate, but every time Soleil looked up from her plate, his eyes met hers. They were nearly finished with their meal when the prince cleared his throat. "I can see why Cherub hosted dinner parties. This is an impressive dining room."

"We only eat in here when Cherub's home," Rosette said. "When it's just us, we eat in the conservatory. That's where the pets are now."

Soleil chimed in. "When Cherub was here and we didn't have guests, we'd all dress in our finest gowns and practice our dinner etiquette around this table."

She could almost see him there, in one of his embroidered three-piece suits, his white hair gleaming with a gel he used to keep his curls in place. They would each demonstrate polite conversation between dainty bites of food. Cherub taught them to be interesting enough to keep their company's attention while not revealing anything too personal. Their statements should be clear and fluid with brief pauses to encourage a response. When she or her sisters did well, Cherub's eyes would shine with his full attention. When they didn't, he would not reprimand them, but his disinterest was clear in the way his gaze wandered to something on the table, as if the dinnerware were more charming than whoever was speaking.

"Over dessert, Cherub would tell us about his wild adventures," Rosette said.

Kai gave a playful smirk. "Wild, huh?"

"Quite," Soleil told him in all seriousness. "Throughout the Dragon Fae Islands and across time."

He choked on a sip of his water. "You're joking."

"Not at all," Rosette said. "Cherub traded his transformation services for a rare pocket watch that could take him to different years, but every time he returned, the year he had just visited was erased from the watch."

He glanced back at Soleil, then to Stella. "Do you believe him?"

"No," Stella answered.

"Yes," Rosette said at the same time. Her head whipped toward Stella. "He showed us the watch!"

"All that proves is that he found a watch with a blank face and spun a tale to explain it."

Kai arched a brow at Soleil, inviting her to weigh in. "Cherub told a lot of fanciful stories," she told him.

Rosette scowled. "He might have embellished at times, but he wasn't a liar."

Stella kept her mouth shut and inspected her plate.

"Did you recover the watch when he passed?" Kai interjected.

"No." Rosette sighed. "Everything was lost at sea. Only his remains returned home."

"Do you believe he was allowed into the Dragon Fae Islands?"

Rosette picked up her glass. "Well, *I* do."

Stella touched a finger to her chin then waved her hand. "If anyone could charm their way across Dragon Fae borders, it would be Cherub. Or Daisy."

There was a bob to Rosette's head as though she approved of the comment. Soleil regretted implying that Cherub was dishonest. He likely was, but in a harmless way. More importantly, her sister was grieving. Stella had mentioned that Rosette was even having some anxiety. Soleil did not want to upset her further.

The doorbell rang, and a muffled voice managed to carry into the dining room. "Delivery!"

Kai stood. "Please, allow me."

When he left, Soleil immediately apologized to Rosette. "I'm sorry about what I said. I meant no disrespect."

Rosette sifted through the remaining vegetables on her plate with her fork. "He truly cared for us, you know. He always did what he thought was best for each of us." Stella's eyes rolled to the side, but Rosette pretended not to notice. She dropped her fork along with the subject, addressing Soleil. "Your husband is so gallant."

"And he looks at you like he can't look away," Stella added in teasing tone.

"He does, doesn't he?" Perhaps he just needed a small nudge in the right direction. Now that she knew he was conflicted, Soleil was happy to oblige.

He returned with a plant that was nearly half as tall as himself. Rosette stood. "I think we have a spot for it in the hall outside the conservatory. This way."

"Prince Kai?" He had one foot through the doorway behind Rosette when Soleil caught his attention. "I'll unpack us. Our room is to the left of the stairs, the second door on the right."

His shoulders drew up as he pivoted with the plant to look back at her. Soleil doubted he would decline. She didn't think he'd want to embarrass her in front of her sisters. If she was wrong, and he asked about staying in one of the guest bedrooms, she would not complain. A second or two passed before he dipped his chin in acknowledgment then followed Rosette to the hall.

Kai

The stairs stretched wide at their base with posts curling away on either side—a mouth grinning at Kai's folly. Every moment he spent with Soleil felt like acquiescence. How could he share a room with her? How could he not, without insulting her or inviting the scrutiny of her sisters? She had to know that.

He had considered claiming not to be tired since he had slept in the carriage. It hadn't been a particularly restful sleep, but no one else knew that. Then again, he couldn't avoid her forever. She was his wife. At some point, they would share a room. For that matter, at some point, she should stop calling him *Prince Kai.*

Two beady eyes glinted in the dark beside his feet. Blaze slipped through the ornate balusters of the railing and trotted up the stairs. At the top, the fox peered down at him, winked, then headed to the left. Kai's feet seemed to move on their own, carrying him up the stairs and straight to Soleil's door.

A second or two after he knocked, Soleil poked her head around the door, then stepped back to let him pass. Unlike the other rooms he'd seen so far, this one wasn't pink. The walls were bright yellow. Orange silk drapes were drawn open, matching the cushions on the window seat and the pillows atop the yellow comforter on the queen-sized bed. One such pillow lay near the door. Blaze curled herself atop it.

"It's not exactly a bed," Soleil said, "but she seems cozy enough." Blaze lifted her head and flicked her tail. "All right, I'll get you a proper one."

Kai chuckled under his breath. Across the room, the closet door was open, and he could see his clothes hanging inside along with Soleil's.

"If you need anything laundered, just put it in the hamper in the closet and it will be cleaned and returned to the hanger."

"By magic, I presume." Kai looked her way, and the air fled his lungs. His eyes raked over her before he could stop himself. Soleil was dressed in a black satin robe that came to the middle of her thigh. Soft ringlets fell loose about her shoulders and down her back. He forced his gaze back to her face. "I could sleep in one of the guestrooms."

A trace of a smile touched her still-glossed lips. "You could, but it is not necessary. The bed is plenty big for two, and there is a dressing screen for privacy."

Kai followed her gaze to where a wicker screen stood in the corner. She waved a hand and the overhead lights dimmed considerably. He could make out her shadowy figure and the outlines of the furniture, but not much more.

"Goodnight, Prince Kai."

Soleil retreated to the bed, circling to the side furthest from the dressing screen. Kai stepped behind the screen and stripped down to his undershorts. He deposited his day clothes in the hamper and moved to the bed, cognizant of how little he was wearing. The mattress was wide, though, and Soleil was nearly an arm's length away, glued to the other side. They could easily sleep without disturbing each other.

C H A P T E R   10

REMEMBERING

Kai

Kai dreamt that the sun never set, its rays following him to the ends of the earth, where no shadowy corner could block its light. When he awoke, his reality gave new meaning to the dream. Soleil's head rested on his chest, and her ringlets swept around them. One golden arm stretched across him, her hand curling at the side of his ribs. Her glossed lips were slightly parted as she snoozed, her breath synchronized with his.

He picked up a spiral curl, smoothing the bronze and gold strands between his fingers. Dropping his nose to the top of her head, he breathed deep. She still smelled faintly of pine and winterberries from home. It was an intoxicating combination: the familiar, homey scent on his foreign wife's unusual form.

Soleil sighed, her breath warm and soft on his chest. His hand stilled in her hair, and he muttered a curse, reigning in the urge to trail his fingertips down the column of her neck. He extricated himself as gently as he could. Soleil rolled to the center of the bed, mumbling something incoherent as she went.

He contemplated her serene expression. She wanted to be married to him. Even after he revealed he had never wanted an arranged marriage, she invited him to stay in her room. Why? Despite his initial assumption, his gut now told him it wasn't because she wanted to be a princess. So, what was it then? Was she not well of mind? Hopelessly insecure? Neither of those possibilities felt right.

Kai went to the closet, noting the door to the room was ajar, and Blaze was gone. He retrieved a pair of black trousers and a dark gray collared shirt and carried them to the adjoining bathroom. After a quick shower, he dressed and returned to the room to find Soleil hadn't stirred. The sheets were twisted around her golden form in much the same way she had been twisted around him. Kai was tempted to return to the bed and untangle her. Instead, he forced himself through the door and headed downstairs.

From the dining room's entryway, Kai first noticed Rosette. She sat at the table with both hands wrapped around a mug, wisps of white steam curling up from the top. There was a weariness in her eyes that did not match her upturned lips as she chatted with others. He entered the room to find that another sister had arrived.

She was taller than Rosette, but not quite as tall as Soleil and Stella, and trimmer than her celestial sisters. Her clothes were all white—terrycloth pants, a tank top, and running shoes. A hair tie was low in the long, straight locks that reached the middle of her back, as if it had worked its way loose from a ponytail. Her hair was a brighter blue than her skin, which was dark and flecked with tiny crystals.

"Phire."

She looked up from where she stood behind Stella's chair, braiding her sister's curls. Her glittering eyes matched her dark skin, and her lips matched the brighter color of her hair. "Prince Kai! Please," she said, nodding toward the table, "join us for breakfast. We have tea and coffee and Rosette's pastries."

A rose gold teapot and copper coffee pot sat on the table between a carafe of cream and jar of honey. Plates of fruit and baked treats were set on either side of the beverages. He took a chair, leaving one open for Soleil between him and her sisters.

"We appreciate the transport you arranged," he said, pouring coffee into a speckled white mug. "Did Prince Gage come with you?"

"He did. I slept on the way here, but Gage is more of a late-night person. He's napping upstairs."

"You've been married for nearly a year, right? What's it like coming back to your childhood home?"

"I come back all the time."

"Me too," Stella told him, her head tugging back from Phire's ministrations. "Even in squall season."

He looked between them. "You're teasing me."

"We're not," Phire told him.

"Well, you *are*," Rosette clarified, "you're just not lying." To Kai, she said, "Some nymphs can direct out-of-body experiences."

"Out of body . . ." Kai repeated slowly. "You mean that your spirit leaves your body?"

Phire dipped her head. "It's a rare talent, but Cherub had mastered it and trained us. We can't go anywhere like he could, but we can come to the Doll House, no matter where we are physically."

He eyed each of them, judging their sincerity. "It's true," Stella told him. "It's how Soleil and I can visit our sisters for Christmas, despite the squalls in the Snow Fae Lands."

Rosette sighed. "I much prefer having everyone here in person, but it's nice to know my sisters can always come home." She tilted her head at him. "Soleil didn't tell you this?"

His smile was humble. "I suppose we are still getting to know each other."

Rosette set down her tea and pushed back from the table. "I'd better check on Lady Thorn. I haven't seen her in a bit."

"She and Pudge were snacking on wildflowers out back," Stella said as Phire secured the last hairpin in Stella's bun.

"Was Blaze with them?" Kai asked.

"I didn't see her." Stella left her chair, and Phire sat down. "We'll leave the window open for Savant, just in case."

"Let's just call the panda Princess," Rosette suggested as they left. "She's too pretty to be called Pudge."

"Savant is my owlet from Cherub," Phire told Kai. "She went with me on my morning run but wanted to stay outside when we returned."

"You didn't happen to see a miniature gold and white fox anywhere on your run?"

"No." When Kai moved to stand, she urged him to stay. "Blaze is fine. Sit and have breakfast."

He paused, uncertain. "She's just a kit."

"One that's been transformed by Cherub," she said, topping off her tea. "He enhances an animal's natural strengths. She'll be sharper than the average fox. Savant will be wiser. Lady Thorn will be more loyal." She lifted her mug in the air. "We should probably keep an eye on that panda, though."

Kai sat back down and reached for a scone. "Probably."

Soleil

Waking up alone was normal for Soleil, but this morning, her husband's woodsy scent lingered on her skin and in her hair as though she had been blanketed by him as much as the comforter they had shared. Her shower had taken longer than usual, lathering herself head to toe in crushed wildflower soap, twice. She would not be able to focus today if she smelled like him.

She donned a gown made of charcoal silk and returned to the bathroom to fix her hair. Blaze sauntered in with a scrap of paper in her mouth.

"There you are." The fox dropped the paper at Soleil's feet. "What's this?" She crouched to retrieve the scrap from the floor. It had been torn from Bloom's local circular and contained half of a pet store ad.

"Yes, you need a bed." Blaze nudged Soleil's hands with her muzzle, and Soleil turned the paper over to reveal a partial article. The only full sentence on the page was from a local innkeeper, gushing about the town's fall aesthetic. She flipped it back to the pet store ad.

"Not a bed? Different food?"

Blaze huffed in exasperation and again nudged her hands. Soleil turned the paper back over, reading the innkeeper's quote out loud. "Autumn in Bloom is so cozy and romantic."

Blaze nodded, stomping one foot on the floor.

Soleil angled her head at the creature. "Are you suggesting that I take the prince into town?" Blaze nodded again. "But not today. Today is the service. Although . . . the service isn't until this evening," she reconsidered.

She had plenty of local coin stashed in her room. Cherub gave them each an allowance for summer and winter breaks, but Soleil and Stella were always stuck in the Snow Fae Lands for winter so never spent theirs. "And this would be a way to spend more time alone with him."

Blaze opened her mouth in something akin to a smile.

Soleil patted the kit on her head. "Pretty, smart, *and* helpful. Aren't you the total package?"

Kai

Conversation with Phire was illuminating. She shared that although she and Cherub weren't close, she cared for him and would miss him. She told him about her sisters and their varied personalities. Like Rosette, she cryptically warned him about Emmie, which only made Kai more curious. Their discussion was cut short when Soleil entered the room, prompting him to stand and pull out the chair beside his. To his dismay, a floral aroma wafted about her, replacing the more familiar scent from home. Worse, her ringlets were pinned into a roll at the base of her head.

Soleil leaned over Phire's chair to hug her sister before taking a seat beside Kai. "Is Emmie here too?" she asked Phire.

"No, but she should be here by early afternoon, in plenty of time for the service." A sigh puffed from her shining blue lips. "Daisy will be late."

"As always," Soleil agreed.

Catching up with Phire as she ate, Kai marveled at how rested and relaxed Soleil appeared—blissfully unaware that she had been wrapped around him in her sleep mere hours ago. He, on the other hand, could think of little else. His skin tingled from the residual feel of her in his arms, and his fingers itched to pull the pins loose from her hair. He found his gaze riveted to the sheen of the lips he'd known only once, on the altar. Her sisters all had the same gloss. Was it a feature of Cherub's magic? Could the shine be wiped or kissed away?

Kai suddenly regretted not waking her this morning. He was being tormented by that brief, physical connection. Soleil should have to remember it, too.

"Prince Kai?" It dawned on him that was the second time she'd addressed him. "I'd like to take the carriage into the village before the service and look for a bed for Blaze. Would you care to join me?"

"Of course." It was an automatic response, but given time to think on it, he still would have said yes. The wife he'd been determined to avoid was becoming addictive, and his general resentment of their situation was wearing thin.

Was it the magic of the Nymph Lands, messing with his head? Maybe it was the supernatural charm of the Doll House. Or was it because her sisters treated him as though they had immediately accepted him as family? Whatever the cause, Kai was finding it harder and harder to dislike the idea of a life with Soleil.

CHAPTER 11

A COUPLE IN BLOOM

Soleil
The Township of Bloom

Sidewalk carts of spiced cider and salted caramel cocoas added a sweet and warm aroma to the crisp air, tickling the nose and planting the thought that just one cup would make everything better. A vendor Soleil had known from school refused her coin and handed her two steaming cups of cider. "It's on me," she said kindly, "and I'm sorry for your loss."

They thanked her, pacing away from the cart to take in the town's Main Street. The buildings were uniform in their colors, made of tan stacked stones and panels of light wood, and topped by copper roofs. Each storefront window featured autumn colors and the occasional pumpkin. Garlands made of silken fall leaves were wrapped around the lampposts that supported hanging baskets of Mums in gold, orange, and purple.

Soleil had directed the carriage to park in a back-alley lot since she was not sure how long they would be, but Kai was amenable to browsing for a bit. Last night, he had been tentative, but this morning, he had been pleasant and engaging. On the ride over, he'd asked her how she slept, if she recalled her dreams, and if she felt well rested. The way he looked at her had become a tad bolder, too. She liked it.

She was tempted to ask him how he was feeling about their arranged marriage now. Ultimately, Soleil opted not to poke at the sore subject. Things were going so well.

Nymphs bustled all around. People she knew personally offered polite greetings and condolences. "You have a lot of friends here," he observed.

"I have a lot of friendly acquaintances from school, but my sisters are my closest friends," she said, then considered that Vynn might be in that closer circle as well. She suspected that Emmie had encouraged him to reach out as often as he did, and if so, Soleil was glad for her sister's intervention. Vynn had become a trusted friend.

"I'm closer with my brothers, too. We all had friends in school, but when you're a prince, it's hard to know who would have been your friend if you weren't," he said, distracted as an older couple walked by, openly gawking at them. "Are they new in town?" he asked her quietly. "Or are they still not used to you and your sisters?"

She grinned. "It's you they're looking at. Bloom is small and out of the way. We don't see many fae here, and even the males have to crane their necks to get a good look at you."

Kai stood a little straighter. They continued along the street, passing a culinary store, a chocolatier, and a tea shop. "This covers Stella and Rosette," he said.

She brightened, pleased that he had learned this much about her sisters on his own. "The bookstore is just across the street. Should we stop in?"

"We don't have time. When I go to a bookstore, I'm there for most of the day." He paced forward. "Where do you shop?"

"Occasionally, I'll purchase new stationery. I enjoy writing letters to my sisters and friends." She glanced up at him. "Unlike you, I am a better writer than speaker." At his apparent confusion, she elaborated. "Years ago, I was at the Winter's End Fair when Emperor Atamai asked you to give an impromptu speech about Icelyn. We were only eighteen then, but you handled it beautifully."

His eyes shifted down the street, glazing in recall. "He just asked me to say a few words. I didn't think of it as a speech." His steps slowed. "Did you know then? That we were betrothed?"

"Yes, but I was asked to keep my distance, since your parents had just passed the year before and our betrothal was contingent upon you not choosing a different bride."

A fact that only added to her consternation when he didn't want her on their wedding day. If he didn't like her, why hadn't he chosen someone else?

"I was twenty-two when I learned of my father's decree. The imperial advisors waited until Atamai was twenty-four to tell us."

She stopped and faced him. "I didn't know that. I only heard of how Atamai refused the bride selected for him and married an elderly fae."

"An elderly fae who was on the verge of passing from this life. He's something of a rebel like that." He chuckled. "I could not find such an option."

"And there wasn't . . . someone special?"

His gaze swept across her face. "No, there was no one. I was considered a young and inexperienced leader. I still am. I had thought I'd be in my forties or fifties before I felt settled enough to look for a wife. If I'd selected a bride before twenty-five, it would have been a farce. I didn't want any part in that."

Hmm. She could not help but wonder how different things could have gone had they been introduced younger—or if Cherub had arranged their marriage in their forties. Might Kai have fallen for her all on his own, just as she had fallen for him?

Was he falling for her now? Or just making the most of their arrangement? How would he feel when he learned of the possible annulment? Given his moral position on arranged marriage, she could envision him asking her to sign it. But here on this casual stroll through her hometown, she could envision him asking her *not* to sign it, too.

Soleil pointed at the next shop over, where a sign shaped like a dog standing with a cat hung by the door. "I promised Blaze a bed."

"So, you did." He opened the door for her.

An array of pumpkin, ghost, and candy corn costumes in all different sizes stood front and center. "These are cute."

The prince cocked his head to the side and brought a hand to his jaw. "I can't imagine Blaze wearing a costume. Pudge maybe, but not Blaze."

"Princess Pudge would make a great pumpkin," Soleil agreed.

On the other side of the costumes were aisles of standard pet care items. Soleil and Kai turned together down the row for beds and blankets. "Large selection for such a small town," he observed.

Soleil found herself nodding in agreement. "I had no idea. We never had pets before. The animals Cherub transformed were all to impress other people."

He walked on, moving past the large beds to the smaller ones. "These look about right. Do you want an oval shape? A square?" His gaze traveled up and down the assortment of tiny beds for her kit.

"Oval, but I'm not sure what color." Soleil stood beside him. "Gold or white would go well with her fur."

"But not so much with the room."

Soleil pursed her lips, reaching for an orange bed at the same time he reached for a silver bed—one that would go well with his room in Icelyn. She stilled, her eyes clashing with his. Kai plucked the silver satin bed from the shelf.

"Were you planning to leave her here?"

A warmth ignited within her, butterflies flitting about her belly. "No," she managed without grinning like an idiot, "the silver is perfect."

He carried the bed to the counter, where Soleil paid with local coins and the shopkeeper slipped the purchase into a paper bag. Kai muttered something about reimbursing her when they returned to Icelyn. Soleil had just laughed, but in her mind's eye, the dreams she'd given up were taking shape again—images of her and Kai and a manor full of happy children. Kai saw a place for her in his life, too, assuming she was returning to Icelyn with him.

The blown glass studio was the last shop on that side of Main Street, sharing an alley with a bakery. She had intended to cross here and take him down the other side of the street, but Kai stopped, gesturing up an extended walkway that led to an administrative building. An engraved slab of granite identified the Nymph Council.

"The council is headquartered in Bloom?"

"No, this is just one of the chapters," she explained. "They have public hearings once a quarter to discuss the concerns of multiple towns in this region of the mountains. It's mostly people airing petty grievances, but some of the cases are interesting."

His mouth curved up. "We have both in Icelyn as well, in our community meetings. The territory is small enough that I've never hired an advisor, so I've been running them myself. You're welcome to sit in."

"I'd like that. I won't make a peep."

His brows pinched together. "How are you going to advise if you don't talk?"

"Advise? Princesses don't usually advise on such matters, do they?"

He chuckled. "Neither do princes, but it seems that if the princess was once an aspiring council member, and her prince never appointed an advisor, she should advise."

She could not stop the grin that stretched ear to ear. He had picked out a fox bed in a color to match his room, and now he was inviting her to advise on community matters. He referred to himself as *her prince*. They were little things, but they were adding up to make all the difference for Soleil.

Kai glanced at the crosswalk that would take them to the other side of Main Street. "Where to next?"

"I want to show you something else," she decided out loud, "off Main Street."

CHAPTER 12

THE GREATEST OF THESE

Soleil

Soleil tugged her prince down the alley, through the carriage lot, and onto a frozen dirt path that wound alongside the river below. The soft rush of the flowing water dimmed the noise of Main Street. The path was well-traveled, but at present, no one else was around.

He let her keep hold of his hand as they moved further from the village. The path turned with the river and the sanctuary came into view, across the water. Vines that had gone brown for fall clung to the rounded blue and gray stones that made up the cottage. White gravel paths split apart, leading up the steps to the front doors and around to the back gardens.

Soleil stopped before the bridge. "The doors to the prayer sanctuary open when someone crosses the bridge and alerts the steward. He and his family live on the grounds, further back." She pointed to a steep and narrow path leading to the water. "If you hop the stones, you can reach the back garden without disturbing anyone."

His forehead crinkled, his eyes traveling along the alternate route. "You're likely to sprain your ankle doing that."

"We haven't yet." She let go of his hand and gathered her skirts.

Two steps down the side path, Kai gripped her elbow. "Be careful."

"*You* be careful," she teased. "I've done this a hundred times."

On the riverbank, he let go and followed her across the water, deftly hopping from one boulder to the next. The path up to the property was a gentler incline, but Kai was again at her side to ensure she did not fall. At the top, a maze of bare shrubs and trees led them to the heart of the sanctuary's gardens. An excitement grew within her as they went. Soleil would never tire of the wonder and divine magic of this place.

An evergreen groundcover crept atop the path. She slowed, sneaking a peek at Kai's face. His brow furrowed as he stood before the clear crystal statue of a dove that hovered in mid-air.

"It's . . ." His voice broke off as he studied the piece. Each detail was precise, from the wisps of the feathers on the dove's wings to the fan of its tail. "I thought nymphs could not compel an object to float or fly?"

"We can't. Only the fae have been gifted with that ability." She stepped closer to the dove. "The story goes that while the early settlers of Bloom were building the village, a massive, blank crystal slab appeared here overnight. A local nymph, Mr. Quinn, felt called to carve it. He worked on it for a full year, determined to get every detail just right. All the while," she explained, nodding toward the strip of the engraved scroll in the dove's beak, "he sang those same words to various tunes."

"The greatest of these is love," he read.

Soleil stood beside him. "Some feared he had lost his mind, but while he worked, the people took care of him, bringing food and water. They brought him blankets to work through the cold and a straw hat to work in the sun. When he carved the last detail, the dove lifted from the ground and has been floating here ever since. Mr. Quinn built the prayer sanctuary next. It is stewarded by his family to this day."

"Did you and your sisters visit weekly?"

"We did, even when Cherub was out of town. Rosette still does." She lowered her voice to a scandalous pitch. "Between you and I, Rosette had a crush on the current steward's son for years. He moved away for school, though, and they lost touch."

Kai grew quiet before his gaze cut to Soleil. "You said no one was close to Cherub. Not even Rosette? It was just her and Daisy and Cherub after the rest of you moved abroad for school."

"Daisy and Cherub weren't around much." A sigh escaped her. "She wanted to be close with him. He made us feel special, but there was always a distance there, too. It was who he was, a part of his mystique. Rosette never gave up hope that she could connect with him."

She left out the fact that she was once like Rosette. The more they reached out, the more Cherub withdrew. Soleil was still young when she quit seeking his affection. Rosette never did.

"She lost that hope when he died," he said absently, his eyes straying back to the dove. "My mother was advanced in age when she had me, and unlike my brothers, I was not planned or expected. I exhausted her. It was clear in her eyes and in every half-hearted hug, but I thought I could win her over by excelling at . . . *everything*. She died, and my father soon followed, but her loss hurt more. All my hopes of being close with her one day had died along with her."

There was a hollowness to his words, as if he were recalling someone else's story, and yet Soleil felt his sorrow deep in her gut. The young prince's accomplishments were well known, but she, like everyone else, assumed the motivator had been his duty to lead. She hadn't known his relationship with his mother had been so strained. Some things could not be learned from textbooks. "I'm sorry."

Kai cleared his throat. "I've made peace with it." He turned on his heel without meeting her gaze. "I assume no one will be disturbed if we take the bridge back?"

He strode away before she could answer, and Soleil watched him go with a heavy heart. Had she touched a nerve that would set them back just as they were becoming close? Or was she fooling herself, making too much of the brief connection?

CHAPTER 13

LOVESICK

Kai

Lovesick was a term from the human days meant to convey a devastating ailment for which there was no cure. Kai once took comfort in the belief that only fools succumbed to this invisible plague, but he was beginning to think even he was not immune. Maybe he was a fool. Who else would confess their deeply personal childhood regret to the one person they had sworn off only weeks ago? Certainly not a wise person.

It could have been worse. He could have suffered that lapse of judgment in front of someone untrustworthy who might share it with someone else. He couldn't explain how he knew Soleil wouldn't, but he knew. His soul knew that he could trust her, and his heart was eager to follow, but his mind held him in check.

On the carriage ride back to the Doll House, Soleil was respectfully silent. Her usually bright and open countenance was downcast, and Kai was the cause. Again, his thoughts returned to the puzzle of why she wanted him.

"*How* can you be okay with a *forced* marriage?"

Soleil flinched at the question that had come out a tad louder and harsher than he had intended. "Pardon?"

"You say that it is not uncommon and that Cherub had arranged all your betrothals with upstanding families, but coming from a well-respected family does not by itself make one noble. What if I were a horrible person?"

Soleil swept him with a look then sat back, watching him through her lowered nymph-lashes. "You aren't a horrible person."

He rolled his eyes. "How could you possibly know that?"

"I've studied you for years, Prince Kai. You are fair and kind to the people of Icelyn. Everyone you employ is generously compensated and treated with dignity and respect. You say you would abdicate your throne to become a scientist or historian, but that isn't true. The people of Icelyn mean too much to you."

A few seconds stretched by while Kai absorbed that. She had taken some time to learn all that about him—time he hadn't spared to learn about her, until coming here. He released the disappointing thought. It wasn't the point.

"But what if I were? What if I were cruel and abusive?"

"Then my sisters and I would find a way to free me." She tilted her head to the side. "Or plot to expose you. Or both. Probably both."

"I'm not joking."

"Nor am I. Together, we're quite formidable." There was a slight lift to her chin. "I have no objections to our marriage."

He scoffed. "Well, you should."

"But I don't," Soleil maintained. "You did. The question is: do you still?"

Kai stared back at her, his foolish pride swelling in his throat and choking the simple answer. This stunning, forthright female wanted him for reasons that were entirely unsatisfactory to his rational mind. Yet, some part of him was fast becoming desperate to accept those reasons—to accept her. His bitterness, however valid, was not the impenetrable steel he'd thought it was. It was mere ice, cold and hard, but defenseless against the warmth of Soleil's presence.

The carriage jostled to a rough halt before the Doll House. Soleil launched forward as the door swung open, her knees bumping into his, her hands braced on his thighs. He grasped her arms to steady her, looking down as she looked up. Their lips were so close that if Kai tilted his head forward, he could capture a kiss. A real one, this time, unlike the sorry excuse for a kiss he gave her on their wedding day.

"Soleil?" Rosette appeared at the open door, carrying a large pot of ice puffs. "Oh!" Her eyes went wide, then shifted to the sky as though she had caught them in some compromising position. "Um, Emmie is here, and we're all gathered in the parlor."

Soleil pushed back from Kai, a lovely shade of scarlet coloring her golden cheeks. He hadn't known her altered skin was capable of a blush. Kai composed himself and exited the carriage, offering Soleil assistance. Her cheeks were still red, and her gaze was averted.

Kai took the plant from Rosette. He eyed the thick green stalks that supported large puffs of ice crystals shaped in perfect spheres. "These are from Prince Wren and Princess Baylee."

Rosette pulled the card from the flowerpot to read it. "They are. How did you know?"

"Ice puffs are rare. They only grow in remote areas of Glacia, where my brother and sister-in-law live."

"I thought I saw another pot of these here somewhere."

That was unlikely. Even in Glacia, they were expensive due to their limited supply.

Soleil made a small clearing of her throat. "We should not, ah, keep the others waiting."

She ducked her head and marched to the house. He wouldn't have guessed she was shy. She had boldly asserted that she had no objections to their marriage, but the blush was far more telling—and something he'd like to explore, soon.

Soleil

A chord had been struck within Soleil that vibrated outward, humming through her bones as she moved into the Doll House. It had been a simple touch, innocent and accidental. The prince hadn't kissed her, but she felt certain that he would have, had they not been interrupted. Soleil wrangled what that could mean into a mental box to be opened at a more appropriate time.

In the parlor, a small wooden chest containing Cherub's remains sat beside a silver hand shovel on the coffee table. Rosette directed Kai to set the ice puffs beside a pot of bright purple lilies and then took her seat beside Stella. Lady Thorn and Princess Pudge lay at their feet.

Emmie sat across from them, wearing a tapered black gown. Grains of fine crystals sparkled in her deep forest skin, but her hair and lips were a brighter green. She had tied her hair in a tightly braided bun at the top of her head, and as usual, not a strand was out of place. A tiger cub with dark stripes through her pale green fur was curled in her lap, bits of tinsel glimmering in her coat. The cub picked up her head to acknowledge Soleil, revealing eyes as bright green as Emmie's hair, sparkling like her sister's emerald namesake.

Kai dipped his chin in greeting. "Hello, Emmie."

Emmie's reply was crisp. "Soleil, Prince Kai."

Soleil refrained from crossing the room to hug her. Emmie found such public displays unseemly; Soleil would have to steal the hug in private. *Mean Green* was harsh, but she was also fiercely loyal to each of her sisters. There was a soft warmth beneath her hardened exterior that was reserved for the people she loved.

"What will you name her?" Soleil asked, referring to the cub.

"Gem."

"What are you going to do if Gem grows to adult size?" Stella asked.

Emmie flashed pearly white teeth. "Terrify everyone who dares come too close."

"You do that anyway," Phire teased, entering the room with Prince Gage. She had changed from her morning running outfit into a fitted black dress, coordinating with Gage in his black suit accented by a dark, brushed gold button-up shirt. The Sun Fae was not as tall as Prince Kai but bulky with muscle. Shoulder-length caramel hair waved away from his tanned face, and his brown eyes were bright with mischief.

"Ladies, it's good to see you all." He gestured toward Emmie with his chin. "Even you, Em."

Emmie replied with an amused smirk.

"Good to see you too, Kai." Gage scanned the room. "Where is Daisy?"

Rosette wrung her hands. "She promised she would be here."

"You know Daisy," Stella put in. "She takes the roundabout route everywhere and gets distracted by shiny things along the way."

Phire rubbed her lips together, glancing away as if the topic exhausted her. Gage moved a hand from her waist to her shoulder to massage it. The pair had been in synch like that since the day they met. Soleil was happy for her sister . . . and maybe just a smidge envious.

Emmie set Gem on the floor and moved to the coffee table. She handed the box and small shovel to Rosette. "You cared for him the most. You should do the honors."

Rosette took them from her, glancing around. "Should we wait a little longer for Daisy?"

Emmie turned, leading the way out of the room. "No."

CHAPTER 14

FAREWELL

Soleil

The early evening sky was dusted gray-blue and textured with smoky tufts of clouds when Soleil exited the Doll House with the others. She and her sisters left their pets inside, except Phire, whose little baby-blue owl landed on her shoulder. Its head rotated to take note of everyone in short, sharp movements until its tiny face rested just above its back, staring at Stella.

"Well, that's creepy," Stella breathed, shuffling to the other side of Soleil.

The group stopped before the circular tree bench, and Rosette opened the box. Upon death, everyone's remains appeared the same: a clear, cylindrical crystal that was flat on one end and pointed on the other. The only way to know who the remains belonged to was to hold the crystal in your palm. Despite knowing this, Soleil couldn't help but scrutinize Cherub's crystal, looking for some indication that it had come from someone with extraordinary power. There was no difference, though. Death remained the great equalizer.

Rosette set the box on the ground, gingerly plucking out Cherub's remains. She straightened, closed her eyes, and bowed her head. Her dark pink brows pulled together in concentration on whatever private sentiment she conveyed. When she lifted her head and opened her eyes, she held it out to Soleil.

The smooth, cool crystal slipped into her hands, and an image of Cherub on her wedding day took shape in her mind. Wisps of lavender streaked his pure white hair to match his suit and top hat. He smiled adoringly at her and wished her a happily ever after.

Soleil was grateful for the vision. It didn't come with the false hope of a younger recollection, when she thought of Cherub as her father. Nor did it come with the sting of the revelation that they would never be close. Rather, it was as if she were seeing a schoolteacher or an advisor—someone who had been instrumental in her life.

Soleil bowed her head and said a brief prayer that Cherub's soul had found peace in the heavens. She handed the crystal to Stella, who closed her eyes, mouthed goodbye, and then handed it to Emmie. Emmie immediately handed the crystal to Phire. Phire whispered a few words Soleil could not make out, then handed it back to Rosette.

Rosette looked to the path that led back to the house and bit her lip, no doubt looking for Daisy.

"It's all right," Phire encouraged. "Go ahead."

Rosette released a shaky breath and then knelt beside the bench, using the hand shovel to plant Cherub's remains inside the ring. When she straightened, a few tears slipped from her eyes. Soleil and the others stepped forward to comfort her. Prince Kai offered her a handkerchief, then froze. They all did.

Soleil felt it before she heard it. The tremor underfoot grew to a foreboding rumble, prompting the group to take two giant steps back from the bench ring just as a fountain of soil erupted from inside it. Three pale wood trunks sprouted, twining together to form one mighty base so thick, it split the bench ring apart. Vine-like branches unfurled from the top, cascading around the tree in a curtain of rose and ivory leaves.

A low whistle preceded the burst of pink sparklers in the early night sky, spelling out Cherub's final message:

FAREWELL, FRIENDS!

UNTIL WE MEET AGAIN,

IVAN CHERUB

Champagne-colored fireworks exploded behind the lettering, then faded. After a minute, the sparkling letters faded too.

"So much for a private service."

Soleil turned with the others at the sound of the new voice. The fading light of the sparklers illuminated Rosette's twin, looking up at the sky. Her skin was a soft, buttery yellow, but her eyes and lips were a peach color. A few peach freckles were sprinkled across the bridge of her nose. She dressed her petite figure in an off-white sweater over a knee-length skirt made of light blue plaid. Her thick white hair was loose, the waves falling to her waist, and a tiny bird hovered in the air above one shoulder, wings a blur.

"I'll bet that was visible all over the world." She dropped her gaze to them. "Don't you think?"

"Daisy!" Rosette crossed to her twin and crushed her in a hug.

CHAPTER 15

WISDOM AND WORRY

"Let's eat in the conservatory." Daisy divided a look between Kai and Gage as they all walked back to the Doll House. "It's less formal but you don't mind, do you? We always eat in the conservatory when Cherub isn't here, and, well—" she broke off, flipping a hand in the air as if gesturing to the fact that Cherub wasn't there.

Phire looped her arm in Soleil's, her owlet taking flight from her shoulder and gliding into the woods. "We can arrange that." They veered away from the others and headed to the kitchen.

An alley of white cabinets topped with shiny pastel pink tiles faced a wall of windows to the expansive patio between the house and the lush forest beyond. The conservatory was just beside the kitchen and had the same view. As a child, when Soleil was feeling out of sorts, she would come to the kitchen for one of Stella's specially blended teas and then curl up beside a window in the beams of the sun or the moon. The herbs and natural light always restored her.

"I arranged sky transports tomorrow morning for everyone but the florals."

"Daisy won't stick around for long," Soleil guessed. "I don't love the idea of Rosette being here all by herself."

"Nor do I. We invited her to stay with us in the Sun Fae Lands for a while."

We. It was a term Soleil longed to use for herself and Kai. She would make the same offer to Rosette or any of her sisters, but Kai would have to agree. It was likely that he would, but they hadn't discussed it. There was a lot they hadn't discussed. She wanted children. Did he? She was encouraged by their town visit, but did that mean he would return to the manor? Share a room with her? She wasn't sure.

"She declined but promised to write regularly." Phire brushed a stray hair from her face. "It will be a bit chaotic in the morning, but there will be a carriage to Icelyn for Kai." She leaned a hip on the island. "Or for you both, if you are returning with him."

Soleil breezed past Phire to the rose gold teapot, wrapping her hands at its base and feigning ignorance. She had never mentioned the current state of her marriage in the letters to any of her sisters and wished they'd all seen that for the hint it was. "Of course, I am returning with him."

Soleil whispered the spell that should ensure plenty of fresh tea for their guests, waiting to feel the teapot warm under her hands. It didn't, probably because she was too distracted to properly concentrate. She gave up and moved to the oven, then realized there was nothing she needed there. Rosette had already baked the bread for the finger sandwiches.

Without magic, she grabbed the serving platters, dinner plates, and teacups from the cabinet and set them on the counter. All the while, Phire said nothing. Soleil moved to the icebox, her limbs growing stiff and heavy beneath the unnatural quiet of the room. She clucked her tongue when the icebox failed to respond to her command to move the ingredients to the trays.

Phire moved to her side. "Stella said this happened to her, too. We were never as magic-savvy as the florals, and living in the fae lands, we've fallen out of practice."

Soleil supposed that was true. Nymphs *could* use magic in the fae lands, but it was generally considered rude unless necessary or invited by a fae to do so. "I was able to unpack and direct the carriage to town with no trouble," she muttered, "but I suppose the kitchen is used to Rosette."

It was known to happen. Nymphs called it the homestead bias. A home wasn't truly sentient, and yet household chores came easier to regular residents than they did to visitors.

"Maybe if we try together?" Phire mouthed the words of the spell, and Soleil joined her. Slowly, the contents of the icebox shifted before them. It took several seconds, but then the ingredients were assembled on the trays in a display of meats, cheeses, fruits, vegetables, and finger sandwiches.

Phire tugged Soleil toward the teapot, and each of them set one hand at its base. The teapot began to warm then disappeared along with the food trays. "Hopefully, those went to the conservatory. Shall we go see?"

"Soleil . . ."

Soleil inclined her head in a silent question. A few beats passed.

"I know," Phire said at last. "I'm guessing you don't want to talk about it, or you would have told me directly, and I know that you will always have a room at the Doll House, but our home is open to you as well."

The compassion in Phire's voice ought to have been comforting, but it wasn't. Phire would not make such an offer without first discussing it with Gage. The idea of her happily married sister discussing Soleil's rocky start to marriage was depressing.

Soleil lifted her chin and squared her shoulders. "You worry too much about everyone else. Emmie always said so."

"I do," Phire conceded, "and you rely too heavily on indirectness."

Soleil arched a brow in challenge. "Meaning?"

"Meaning that if you truly want to mend a rift between yourself and Kai, you should tell him plainly what you want out of your marriage."

Soleil rocked back on her heels as she took in her sister from head to toe. "I am to take advice from someone whose marriage was perfect from the start? As if you have any idea what it is like to be in my place?"

Phire did not shrink from the observation. "I hope that you would consider advice from someone who loves you."

The fight deserted Soleil instantly, her shoulders dropping. She loved Phire too, even if it was difficult to be around her and Gage. Phire moved past the kitchen island to stand before her. "Kai has a pure heart. You've always known it, and I see it too, but don't—" Phire stopped herself, amending her words mid-sentence. "I *hope* you won't sweep this under the rug. He needs to understand how his actions have hurt you, even if you have already forgiven him." Phire picked up Soleil's hand, covering it in hers. "Soleil, you deserve mutual respect and shared understanding. We all do."

Soleil bit her lip and nodded, her eyes stinging from the truth. She wanted Kai, wanted him to want her in return, but Phire's advice was sound. If they had any hope of a lasting union, they would need to be direct and honest with each other.

Phire turned, searching the kitchen. She found a small cloth that hung from the oven door and brought it back to her sister, dabbing at the tears.

"I hate that you're always right." Soleil sniffed. "It's annoying."

Phire awarded her with a lopsided smile. "Yes, I know. Emmie tells me all the time."

CHAPTER 16

TWO PRINCES

Kai

If anyone had guessed what to expect of the memorial service for Ivan Cherub, Kai wagered they'd be way off. As they left the garden, he wondered if Cherub had been with them in spirit. Did he see Rosette's tears? Phire's sad but restrained goodbye? Did he see how the others had let him go long before he had passed? Did he have any regrets? Or was he at peace with it all?

Daisy halted at the edge of the flower-lined patio. "Isn't it funny how when someone dies, people send things that will also die in a few weeks?" Kai thought it safe to assume that Daisy was not deeply wounded by her guardian's loss. She gestured with a hand to the conservatory. "There are more in there?"

"As many as we could fit," Rosette confirmed.

He and the others filed into the conservatory behind Daisy, shedding their cloaks and dropping them on a table beside the door. The ceiling and three walls were made of crystal-clear glass. Flowers and potted plants filled the room, bathed in the ethereal glow of the moonlight. Rosette waved a hand, and the room brightened as paper lanterns on each table warmed to life.

The sisters took chairs at the center tables, Stella and Emmie sitting a chair away from Daisy and Rosette, engaged in their own quiet conversation. A pot of tea materialized on the center table along with trays of food set beside stacks of ceramic teacups and small plates.

Gage and Kai filled their plates with food and took them to a standing table along one glass wall. Gage's light brown eyes darted to Daisy and Rosette. "The florals keep my wife up at night," he said quietly. "Phire doesn't want Rosette to be here alone. I'll have to send someone I trust to check up on her."

Kai hummed with a nod. "She's taking Cherub's loss hard. Daisy seems to be doing all right, though."

"Daisy is unpredictable. Phire worries she'll wander into the wrong place, say the wrong thing to the wrong people, and never be seen or heard from again."

Kai knew almost nothing about Daisy, and yet he understood that concern. "I thought she was married to Jameson?"

"For now. They married just before you and Soleil, but they're more like roommates, sharing a house on the east coast," Gage explained. "No one knows what Daisy will do next, least of all Daisy."

Kai turned toward him, curious. Divorce was rare among fae and nymphs alike, but Gage made it sound likely or even inevitable, where Daisy was concerned.

"That's the downside to arranged marriages. You can't be sure the bride and groom will be a good fit. Not that I'm complaining." His attention shifted to the entryway as his wife walked in with Soleil. "Look who I'm married to."

Gage clapped him on the shoulder and left him, joining Phire and Soleil. The appearance of Kai's golden bride cast the rest of the room in shadow, the chatter fading. She carried herself with a composed grace, at ease in the conversation with her sister and brother-in-law. Phire smiled at something Gage said, and Soleil responded with a soft, melodic laugh that made Kai's insides melt.

Look who I'm married to.

"I've been asked not to scare you away."

Kai startled. He hadn't seen Emmie come up beside him.

"But I think we should talk. I'll do my best to stick to the facts and keep my opinions to myself."

She was the same height and build as Phire, taller than Rosette and Daisy but shorter than Soleil and Stella. Her bun looked uncomfortably tight, although it did not appear to bother her. Her deep forest eyes were sharp, locked on him with unwavering intention.

"I don't scare easily," he advised her. He had, in fact, been intrigued given the warnings from Soleil's other sisters. "I'd love to hear your opinions."

CHAPTER 17

EMMIE KNOWS BEST

Kai

Emmie took a half step back, sizing him up and preparing for battle. "Wherever should I start?"

"With Cherub?"

"Cherub was a silly, self-absorbed nymph who just happened to be a genius with magic. He could have lived a full two hundred years if he weren't prone to foolishness, but he died at seventy, manning a boat he's sailed a thousand times."

Kai had wondered how old Cherub was, but because the aging process was suspended between the ages of thirty and one hundred fifty, it was difficult to tell. "Do you believe he could time travel?"

"He could never prove it, but yes, I do." At Kai's obvious surprise, she explained, "For all his flaws, he wasn't an outright liar."

That made two in favor of Cherub's claim to time travel and two against. He wondered what Daisy and Phire thought of it. "How do you feel about the betrothal he arranged for you?"

"He's a Duke in the Sun Fae Lands and meets my primary requirements: intelligent and introverted."

"Hm." He glanced toward Daisy and Rosette. "What do you think about those two?"

"Rosette is an eternal optimist with a bleeding heart. She put Cherub on a pedestal. It will take time, but she will be all right. Daisy barely passed in school and hasn't the sense to think before she speaks or acts, but most people find her charming. She always ends up just fine despite my sister's concerns." She gestured with her head to where Phire stood with Gage and Soleil. "My twin is more like a mother than a sister. She gives sage advice to others but is prone to overthinking, which begets worry."

Kai didn't know why her sisters were so concerned about Emmie talking to him. He found her bold assertions refreshing. "And Stella?"

A smile tugged at Emmie's glossy green lips as her gaze shifted to the table where Stella sat with Daisy and Rosette. "Stella is an excellent herbalist. In that, she is meticulous. In everything else, she is well-meaning but forgetful." She tapped a finger to her temple in emphasis. "Careless."

He chuckled under his breath. "If I asked the others what they thought of you, what would they tell me?"

"That I'm overly critical, unnecessarily harsh, and have a tendency to poke at matters that might be better left alone." Her eyes drifted across the room. "Which brings us to Soleil. She holds herself to the highest of standards while expecting little from others. Stella blames Cherub for that." Kai followed her gaze to where Soleil stood talking with Phire and Gage. "When we were little, Soleil and Rosette thought of Cherub as our father. The more they sought his attention and praise, the more distant he became. Soleil figured out young that he would never change, so she did. She learned to re-focus her energy elsewhere—us, school, her classmates."

Kai's smile dropped. The image of a young Soleil formed in his mind, reaching out to her guardian, only to meet continual disappointment. She hadn't mentioned that when they had discussed Rosette.

"It's a cautionary tale, *Prince Kai*." His head swiveled back toward Emmie at the sharpness in her tone. "Her patience may seem unending, but I assure you, it is not. When it eventually runs out, the damage to your relationship, or lack thereof, will be irreversible. She may forgive you, but no olive branch or apology will revive the affection she so clearly has for you now."

He blinked. Affection? To be amenable to their marriage was one thing. The earlier blush hinted at her attraction to him, but affection? The very idea wrapped around his heart and squeezed tight, eliciting hope and doubt in equal measure. It couldn't be true. He'd done nothing to earn it.

"Don't pretend to not know what I am talking about; it is beneath you." She folded her arms. "Word of how you have humiliated my sister by leaving her on your wedding night has traveled all the way to the Sun Fae and Nymph Lands."

As quickly as it had come, his hope fled, the blood draining from his face. "Humiliated?"

She sketched an imperious brow. "What would you call it?"

Kai had no response. Days ago, he might have called it a peaceful protest—his quiet resistance to an antiquated practice. He had been so consumed by his disdain for his forced marriage.

Even when his anger was fresh, he had not wanted to humiliate Soleil. He should have considered that would be a natural consequence, though, and that her sisters would learn of it. His voice came out low. "She told you she was humiliated?"

"No, she would never," Emmie said in a way that indicated he ought to know that. "Vynn told me."

Every fiber of his being locked tight. "Vynn . . . Vynn *Marius*?"

"Yes, he is a friend of mine from law school. He has assured me that he is keeping in close contact with Soleil and offering his support however he can."

That couldn't be accurate. His staff knew that Kai didn't care for the lawyer. If Marius had visited his home, they would have alerted him. Soleil started toward them, a deep V between her bronze brows.

He turned back to Emmie. "What do you mean, close contact?"

Emmie scoffed. "My advice to you, Prince Kai, is to determine whether this is a marriage you wish to salvage while Soleil still cares about what you think because ultimately, the choice is hers, not yours."

CHAPTER 18

FIREWORKS OF ANOTHER KIND

Soleil

Watching an outsider converse with Emmie was like watching a child reach out to pet a sleeping tiger. The tiger might be undisturbed, but who in their right mind would take that chance? When Soleil first noticed them together, all seemed fine, but by the time she politely excused herself from Phire and Gage's company to make her way toward them, her prince's handsome face had drawn into a dark expression.

She stopped before them just as Emmie dispensed her advice. Tension radiated from Kai's stock-still body. "What is she talking about?" he asked her.

Emmie drew up, also looking to Soleil. "He doesn't know about the annulment option?"

"*Annulment option?*"

Daisy's gasp pierced the room. "You didn't tell him?" All eyes turned to where she sat with Rosette and Stella, astonished. "That's pretty brutal, given your status. You're not just high society, you're royalty. This is the stuff major scandals are made of. If you don't get ahead of this—"

"I think they get it," Stella cut in.

If looks could kill, Soleil wasn't sure who would perish under Kai's harsh gaze first, Emmie or Daisy. He pivoted to Soleil, speaking through clenched teeth. "Care to explain?"

Phire hooked one arm around Gage's bicep and lifted a palm in the air, urging the others to follow them out. "Why don't we give these two some privacy?"

Daisy popped out her lower lip. "We haven't had dessert yet. It's not like *not* eating will help."

"We'll have dessert in the parlor," Rosette suggested with a gentle push at Daisy's back.

Soleil clasped her hands before her and watched her sisters go. She drew in a breath through her nose and summarized the matter. "Rosette inherited the Doll House, but the Nymph Council could find no records of our adoptions. Cherub technically did not have the right to enter us into our betrothal contracts. Because the betrothals are legally void, the council will grant an annulment to those of us who have already married if we want one."

When the prince did not respond, she turned to find he had moved to the back door and was crouched over a pot of ice puffs. She crossed to him, and he stood, a small card pinched between his thumb and forefinger. Soleil's name was neatly printed on the envelope.

"If Vynn Marius is Emmie's friend from school," he began, a steel edge creeping into his voice, "why is he sending flowers to you?"

Just behind him, a second card protruded from the plant. That one had Emmie's name on it. "Vynn is my friend as well," she said, wondering what this had to do with anything. "We became close in the months leading to the wedding."

His teeth grated together. "How close?"

She drew back, taking him in with wide eyes. His posture was rigid. There was an angry slant to his dark brows. Soleil's mouth dropped open, but no words came out. When the laughter bubbled forth, she did not try to stop it.

Her uncertain prince was jealous.

Kai

The melody of Soleil's laughter should have been a welcome sound, but Kai could not appreciate her sense of humor at that moment. In fact, he was tempted to cram an ice puff in her mouth. He waited. It took a minute. Finally, she brought one hand to her belly and lifted the other to her face, wiping tears from the corners of her eyes.

"Are you through?"

"I think so." Another small giggle slipped out before she took a steadying breath. "Yes, I think—I think I'm good."

"I fail to see the humor."

She grinned up at him. "Despite the magnitude of what I have relayed, you choose to focus on an innocent card from a friend who happens to be male? It's ridiculous."

"I don't care how many male friends you have," Kai informed her, "but why Lord Marius would be among them is beyond me."

"Vynn? He's been so kind."

"As someone who grew up with him, I can assure you he is not always genuine. And stop calling him that. If you can't call me *Kai* without the 'prince,' you don't get to call him *Vynn*."

She sobered, her lips rubbing together as she considered him. "I address you as Prince Kai because you've never invited me to drop the formality," she said quietly, "but I would rather call you Kai."

His eyes searched hers. "I would rather you call me Kai, too."

Soleil stepped back from him, looking around the conservatory as she seemed to gather her thoughts. When she faced him, her shoulders rolled back. "It is ironic that you object to arranged marriage because you think it isn't right, but then left me alone and unsupported as a new princess. How is that right?"

He inhaled sharply. It should be a rhetorical question—the answer was obvious—but it was a fair question, too, and Kai felt he owed her the answer. "It isn't."

"No, I don't think so either." She released a heavy breath. "Your reputation as prince will not be tarnished if our marriage is annulled. It is an unfortunate situation, but no one's fault. It is true that the annulment only requires my signature, but I am giving you the choice— one that you weren't given before."

Kai's gut twisted. Her offer brought him no relief. On the contrary, it was hurtful that she would be willing to let him go, which was absurd considering his behavior thus far.

"As much as I want this marriage to work," she said, her warm eyes piercing his soul, "it won't unless you want it too."

He swallowed. Peering down at the card in his hand, he forced his grip to relax. What was wrong with him?

"You're right," he muttered. "This is ridiculous."

He couldn't bring himself to look back at her as he moved to the door, dropping the card back into the ice puffs and grabbing his cloak. Outside, his wings materialized by his silent command, passing through the inconspicuous slits cut into all his clothes. They unfurled in a majestic display of the palest, silvery blue. Launching upward, Kai soared into the clouded night sky and headed to the Snow Fae Lands.

CHAPTER 19

ADJUSTING

Soleil

Nymph Lands

Soleil's affirmation sailed through the fragrant air of her bedchamber and dissipated before it reached the window where it might have turned into something as hopeful, and as futile, as a wish.

"No matter," she whispered to herself. "I will adjust."

The night before, she'd said nothing to her sisters after the prince had left, retiring to her room alone. Blaze had taken pity on her, foregoing the new bed to curl up at her side. Soleil could not sleep much, though. She'd spent most of the night replaying the limited moments she'd had with Kai over the past two days.

They shared a genuine chemistry. It was the spark of something pure, something that was meant to be much more. She just didn't know if it was enough.

It was still dark out when she awoke, sitting up in an empty bed. Even Blaze had abandoned her. The kit probably needed a break from the air of depression that no doubt filled the room.

She headed to the shower, hoping the steam and fresh, floral soap might help soothe her nerves. Instead, she found herself wondering if she would ever again wear the scent of the frosted pine and winterberries of Icelyn. From her closet, she selected an old outfit she'd had since college—a fawn brown skirt topped by a pale peach camisole and matching cardigan. As she dressed, she stared at Kai's clothes hanging beside hers in the closet.

She reminded herself that she had given him a choice. It was unreasonable to expect him to make such a critical decision without first giving it some thought. When she'd made the offer, she hadn't considered what she would do with herself in the meantime. That much was clear to her now, though. She could not return to Icelyn until Kai was sure of what he wanted.

Soleil uttered a spell to pack his clothes. In a blink, the garments disappeared from the hangers, his suitcase materializing before the closet. Her own suitcase remained on the closet's floor, empty. She spun the band of blue and white diamonds around her finger. It felt heavier. She dreaded the idea of wearing it while they were separated as much as she hated the idea of ever removing it.

The door creaked open, prompting Soleil to spin around. Blaze trotted in, and her chest deflated. "Oh," she said, crossing the short space to close the door, "it's just you."

Blaze paused to swish her tail with an indignant sniff, then continued into the room. She retrieved her new pet bed and carried it in her mouth to set it beside Kai's suitcase. Soleil exhaled on a sigh. "It is perfect."

She could picture the silver satin piece in their bedchamber in Icelyn, at the foot of their bed, or in one of the wide windowsills. They could carve a pet entrance into the balcony door. Blaze would come in from the cold and join them by the fire. Kai would be in the oversized chair before the fireplace, reading some dusty old journal, while she curled at his side, reading letters from her sisters.

But if Kai couldn't envision it too, it would never happen.

She wished she had kissed him in the carriage before Rosette had interrupted. It might have been her last opportunity for a real kiss—one they both wanted rather than the one they had for show on their wedding day. Soleil swallowed as her head dropped forward. "I'm sorry, Blaze." She picked up the bed and returned it to its original place. "I think we'll be here for a while."

A knock sounded from the hall, too soft to be Kai, and yet Soleil hoped it was him anyway. She opened the door to Rosette and Lady Thorn.

"I thought you might be up," Rosette said quietly. "No word from Prince Kai?"

Soleil didn't know how Rosette knew, but there was no sense in denying he was gone. Stepping aside, she waved her sister into the room. "I'm giving him time. I'll be staying at the Doll House for now."

Rosette's dark pink mouth tugged downward. "You're not returning to Icelyn?"

"We've barely talked since I've been back. This gives us more time to catch up."

"You'll be stuck outside of the Snow Fae Lands for the squall season if you don't go now."

That was likely true. Although there were occasional breaks between squalls, they were short and unpredictable. "Or I'll be stuck inside them with a husband who does not want me."

A crease of doubt appeared at Rosette's forehead. "He doesn't act like he doesn't want you."

"If that were true, he'd be here." She tossed her head, shaking the thought from her brain. "Enough about me. I've been self-absorbed since I arrived. How are you? Stella says you have been feeling anxious."

Rosette gave the barest of nods, scooping up Lady Thorn and sitting at the edge of the bed with the wolf pup in her lap. "Sometimes, and just a little. I'll be all right. It is strange to know that he'll never be coming home.

Eventually, no one will. You'll all be married, and it will just be me and Lady Thorn in the Doll House. Cherub said he was working on the right match, but . . ."

Soleil sat beside her. "Rosette, any eligible bachelor would be lucky to have you. We're only twenty-five. There is plenty of time to choose a husband."

"I suppose." Her gaze dipped to the floor. "I know he wasn't around much, but I'm going to miss him. However he came to be our guardian, he always did what he believed was best for us."

Soleil wasn't sure what to say to that. Where they all came from was the least of her concerns. No biological relatives were knocking down their door, and Cherub provided well for them. She wasn't sure he always did what was best for them, though. He knew Rosette wanted to marry. There were plenty of noble, educated, well-established nymphs who would want her as a wife. So, why didn't he arrange it? He could have left the Doll House to Stella instead. She had never wanted to marry.

"Daisy thinks he may have brought us all here from another time."

That hadn't occurred to her, but then, she didn't believe he could time travel.

Rosette scratched Lady Thorn behind the ears, and the little pup leaned her head into her hands. "I know you and Stella don't believe all his stories, but if anyone *could* do it, it would have been Cherub."

Soleil breathed a half-hearted laugh. "Well, you have us there."

At his service, Soleil had made peace with the role Cherub had played in her life, but she didn't think she would ever share Rosette's unwavering admiration. She would likely always have questions, always have doubts. Soleil wasn't sure if that was because she was a little jaded or if Rosette was a little naïve.

Rosette glanced toward the window. "The sun will be up soon, and everyone will be heading out."

Soleil covered a yawn. "I'll come down and say goodbye."

"You don't have to." She stood from the bed and set Lady Thorn on the floor. "I can send your breakfast up here and tell them you're not to be disturbed."

It was a tempting offer, but one Soleil had to decline. "No, I want to see everyone before they go. They should hear from me why I'm staying."

CHAPTER 20

SON OF A CUCKOLD EMPEROR

Kai

Glacia, Snow Fae Lands

Glacia lay on the other side of Kanamori proper from Icelyn where the ice was a shade more green than blue, gleaming with aquamarine. Marius lived in an apartment downtown but according to the landlord, he was visiting his uncle. Kai knew the place; everyone did. The palatial abode was carved high into the side of an ice cliff. Natural frozen columns framed the home's wall of windows.

It was midafternoon when Kai landed at the edge of the narrow bridge over a chasm of ice crystals. A horse-drawn carriage was waiting just behind him, a footman standing at attention at the carriage door. Kai strode forward. He was halfway across the bridge when Marius walked through the front door, looking as though he had just bathed. His blond hair was damp and combed back, and his beard was neatly trimmed.

Marius looked up and froze mid-step. "Kai?"

"Lord Marius," he greeted, removing his cloak and dropping it to the ground. "My wife received your flowers and card, but I thought it best to respond in person."

Kai's suit jacket followed his cloak. A steely glint entered Vynn's eyes. They remained fixed on Kai as he set his briefcase down in the snow. "We're friends. Nothing more. I swear it."

"I know. She told me as much, and I have no reason to doubt her." Kai rolled up his sleeves on his forearms. "But I take issue with your advances, given our history."

"Our fathers' history, not ours." Vynn shed his cloak and coat. "There were no advances."

Kai raised his fists. Physically, they were about evenly matched. They had both trained with the imperial guard, and Kai was only a shade taller. Despite their past, they had never gone to blows, but when they were friends, Kai had sensed Vynn would love nothing more than to take a swing at him. Back then, he had dismissed it as unexercised adolescent energy. He'd been wrong.

"Come on, this is your chance. Take your best shot at a son of the *cuckold emperor*."

Vynn winced at the reminder of the taunt that followed Kai throughout school; the one that Vynn himself had spread while pretending to be Kai's friend. He held up one hand. "If you're here to thrash me for being the world's worst friend, fine—it's long overdue—but I've done nothing improper toward Soleil. I would never."

"No?" Kai stepped forward. "You befriended her without ever visiting my home. You knew my staff would alert me if they knew."

His blue eyes widened before he shook his head. "If I thought you'd care, I would have visited every day. Soleil deserves better."

Kai smashed his fist into Vynn's jaw as the last words left his mouth. Vynn responded with a jab to Kai's ribs, then dropped when Kai brought a knee to his stomach. He hauled himself back up and lunged for Kai, catching him around the midsection and driving them into the bridge with a thud.

They rolled atop the iced structure, exchanging blow after blow. Kai could not track who landed more hits, but for each he took, he came back strong with his own. Finally, Vynn shoved himself away.

"Enough!" He rolled to his back to catch his breath. "You have good reasons to hate me," he rasped, "but I swear to you, Soleil is not one of them."

Kai took a moment to steady his breathing. "That might be comforting if you weren't known to lie."

"I'm not that person anymore," he said, sitting up. "You think it is worse to be the third son of someone who was wronged? Or the only son of someone who did wrong?"

Kai opened his mouth, then snapped it shut. It was well known that Vynn cut ties with his father when he left the Snow Fae Lands to study abroad. He earned a good salary as Wren's advisor, but it was a pittance compared to the family fortune he had lost. Kai had known this. It was easy to lump Vynn in with his father and despise the whole family, but Vynn's father would never have walked away from that money for anything or anyone.

"There was nothing I could say or do to make things right, so I fell in line and acted the way everyone expected—everyone except you. I regret it, deeply, but I cannot change it. We can't go back."

Kai scanned his face. He appeared sincere enough, and Kai found himself empathizing. He had a few regrets of his own lately.

He offered a hand to his former friend, pulling him to his feet. Kai turned away, searching for his coat and cloak and spotting them on the bridge nearby. "Stay away from my wife, and we'll call it even."

It was conspicuously silent behind him as he picked up his clothes. Kai turned back to find Vynn hadn't moved. "I . . . can't." He lifted his palm in a *hold on* gesture, but Kai charged forward. "Wait—"

Kai knocked the wind out of him, cutting off his words as the two toppled over the side of the narrow bridge. Their wings sprang open automatically, slowing their fall toward the jagged ice crystals of the chasm. Still, they fought. Kai landed two uppercuts, and Vynn came back with a punch to the gut, the force of which knocked their descent off course. They sailed to the side, Vynn's back hovering just inches before a spike that could have been lethal. The feuding fae exchanged a wide-eyed look and soared upward together, landing back on the bridge.

Vynn swore softly under his breath. "You're going to kill us."

Kai caught hold of his collar, raising his fist again.

"Emmie!" Vynn hollered. Kai paused with his fist mid-air. "Because of Emmie!"

Kai let him go, and Vynn bent forward, his hands on his thighs as he took another gulp of air. "She asked me to look after Soleil, and I promised I would."

Kai sneered, "You can tell Emmie that Soleil's *husband* is looking after her."

Vynn shook his head, his gaze cast to the ground. "You don't understand."

"What?" Kai snapped.

His face crumpled into an expression Kai could only describe as agony. Kai clenched and unclenched one fist at his side as he watched the lawyer. That Vynn made no attempt to reply was telling. It wasn't like him not to have the right words. "So, you *are* after someone's bride, just not mine."

"*Intended* bride, and I would have never acted on it," Vynn said. "Her reputation is too important to me, but now . . . everything has changed."

Kai turned away. The marriage he'd done nothing but complain about could be erased by Soleil with a simple signature. Yet, she was giving the decision to him even though he had treated her terribly from the start. She should want—no, *demand*—more for herself. In that, Kai and Vynn agreed: Soleil deserved better.

He heaved a breath, shaking out his wings and stretching them wide.

"Kai," Vynn called after him. "Are we good?"

He looked over his shoulder. "Are you in love with Emmie?"

Vynn closed his eyes briefly as if it pained him to admit it. "I have been for years."

"Then we're good." He waved a dismissive hand in the air. "That's punishment enough."

CHAPTER 21

WHAT A NYMPH WANTS

Soleil
The Doll House

After assuring each of her sisters that she would be all right and stealing that rare hug from Emmie, Soleil returned to her room. She collapsed on the bed and slept for hours. Her dreams flipped from being all alone in the Icelyn manor to living all alone in the Doll House. In both, she walked into oversized, empty rooms, calling out to ask if anyone was there and hearing only her echo in reply.

The low howl of the wind accompanied a blast of cold air, jolting her awake. She was certain her window had been closed when she went to sleep, but now it was wide open, her curtains blowing up and snapping down. Her mouth went dry and her heart hammered in her chest as she scrambled out of the bed. When Kai appeared, she brought a hand to her chest, her adrenaline colliding with awe. His dark hair whipped about his face, his ice blue wings flexing then folding behind him.

"You scared me half to death!"

His wings disappeared as he climbed through the window and closed it. When he sank into the window seat, she took in the state of his face. A crescent of purple underscored his eye. His lower lip was swelling, and an angry red line split the side. "What happened to your face?"

He stretched his jaw. "I'm fine."

"You're *not* fine. Who did this?" she repeated.

"That's not important."

"It's important to me!"

Kai regarded her through lowered lashes. "It shouldn't be." His tone was soft with regret. Looking past the battered state of his face, she searched for the cause. Did he regret leaving her last night? Or did he regret that what he had come to say would be hurtful? That Soleil couldn't guess made her wary.

His gaze traveled over her, then shifted to the room, landing on the open closet. His suitcase no longer sat before it. She had directed it to the sky scamp upon its arrival, and judging by the position of the sun behind Kai, the transport had likely come and gone. He had to notice, though, that his clothes were missing from the hangers.

"Did you change your mind while I was gone?"

She drew a breath through her nose. "I have decided that I will stay here for the time being. Squall season will begin soon, and I do not wish to be stuck with someone who is not sure whether they want me."

Kai stared at her for so long she thought he might not have heard her. Perhaps his ears were ringing. "That's . . . sensible."

She gave a brisk nod, smoothing the front of her skirt with her hand. "I did not know you were returning, so I sent your things with the sky scamp back to Icelyn."

"The scamp is still here, waiting."

"Oh. Then your suitcase is there, waiting with it." She took one small step toward him, wanting to press him for details of what had happened, but then thought better of it. If he ultimately decided to annul the marriage, those details were none of her business. "Everyone knows that Cherub has passed. If someone were to inquire, it is reasonable to tell them that I am staying with my sisters until the end of squall season."

"Reasonable," Kai echoed, his voice hollow.

Soleil closed the distance between them, summoning an ice pack as she went, grateful that it came to her on the first command. "Here," she told him, lifting the pack to his eye.

He wrapped a steady hand around her wrist before she could reach his face. "Are you giving up on me? Like

Cherub?" Soleil tilted her head on a frown, and Kai continued, his voice low and monotone. "Emmie told me. She said you once loved him like Rosette did. You wanted his affection, but he pushed you away, and you gave up." His hand dropped away from hers. "I don't blame you for either. You deserve better than what we have given you."

Soleil could not tell if he was expressing an apology or a mere confession. "Emmie was quite chatty last night," she muttered, lifting the ice to his eye again. This time, he let her. "Yes, there was a time, as a child, that I was much like Rosette. Then I realized that he wasn't my father and never wanted to be. I had to accept that." A tinge of sadness highlighted her words when she added, "If you don't wish to be my husband, I will have to accept that too."

"Soleil . . ." her name came out on a tortured rasp. "You have every right to send me away, but I don't want to leave without you."

Her breath caught in her throat, her pulse accelerating. She lowered the ice pack, scanning his face. "You don't?"

He gave a slow shake of his head. "No. What you said to me last night . . . you're right, and I'm ashamed that I needed to hear it. Leaving you on our wedding night was inexcusable."

She was torn between feeling relieved and remaining cautious. "Do you want me to return to Icelyn because you feel badly for being rude or because you want this marriage?"

"No, Soleil, I don't want this marriage. I want to start fresh." He captured her hands in his. "Tell me what you want—from me, from our life together."

The softness of his voice, coupled with his intense focus, emboldened her. Phire's advice rang in her ears. Soleil needed to be clear about what she wanted, and she needed to clearly understand what Kai wanted, too. "I want you to treat me like the wife you want, not the burden you were saddled with." Her gaze skimmed the floor as she realized that was in fact what their arranged marriage was to him. "I know that technically I was, but—"

"No," he interjected. "You were never a burden." He gave her hands a gentle squeeze. "Tell me what else you want."

"I want . . ." She hesitated for a second, then blurted, "Children. I want children. Lots of them."

His dark brows inched upward then smoothed out as he breathed a laugh. "Of course you do." He shook his head to himself. "You'll make a wonderful mother. What else?"

Tears pricked her eyes. This couldn't be real. It was too close to her daydreams and too far from her reality. "I . . . want . . ." She swallowed through the lump in her throat. "I want you to kiss me," she whispered as a tear trickled down her cheek. "Kiss me, and then I'll know if this is real."

Kai rose to his feet, brushing the tear away with his thumb. He slipped his hand to the base of her neck and lowered his mouth to hers. The kiss was slow and deliberate, liquifying her limbs. When their lips broke apart, Soleil's head was spinning.

"I want those every day," she breathed.

He gave a low chuckle. "Done." Lifting a hand to her face, Kai gently brushed his knuckles along her jaw. "What else?"

"My sisters—if they ever need us, I want to know you will be there for them, too."

"As if they were my own flesh and blood."

"That's it," she said, leaning into him. "That's all I want."

"You're letting me off easy," he chided. "And you will promise to tell me when I'm out of line?"

"I will." Soleil wrapped her arms around his waist and beamed up at him. "What else?"

His fingers slipped into her hair. "Will you wear your curls down like this, whenever we are alone together?" He dropped his nose to the top of her head. "And only wear scents from Icelyn?"

A small laugh slipped from her lips. "Yes. What else?"

He hummed to himself, thinking. "I promise to tell you when you have accosted me in your sleep."

She squinted back at him, not understanding. "When I . . .?"

"The other morning when I awoke in your bed, you were sprawled atop me."

Her gaze strayed to the bed, then back to Kai. "I was not."

"You were," he said, his eyes going round in mock innocence. "It was quite shocking."

Her cheeks warmed with a blush. "You're teasing me."

"I assure you, I am not. I had to pry myself loose."

A nervous laugh weaseled its way through her words. "Stop it!"

"I'm not complaining." He smoothed the back of one finger down the side of her cheek. "I didn't know your skin was capable of this blush until yesterday. I've been dreaming of all the ways I might bring it back." Soleil's cheeks went from warm to hot. His gaze lingered on her mouth, and he drew the pad of his thumb over her lower lip. "This gloss will never come off? No matter how much I kiss you?"

"No, but you are welcome to try."

Kai wove his hands in her hair and kissed her. He lifted his head then brushed his lips over hers once more.

Soleil leaned back, visually tracing his face. "I should have told you about the annulment. I'm sorry."

"I understand why you didn't."

"Still, we should not keep secrets from each other."

"No, we should not."

"I'm glad you agree." She cupped the uninjured side of his jaw. "Who did this?"

He dropped his head back with a groan. "Clever, wife. Very clever."

"Who?" she pressed.

"Lord Marius," he grumbled, "but he looks worse than I do."

Her eyes flew wide. "You didn't."

"I did, and I'd do it again, but I don't think I'll have to."

"Kai," Soleil said evenly, "Vynn's my friend."

"I know, and I'm fine with it, but we had other things to discuss." He gave her a pointed look. "And he's still *Lord Marius* to you. Don't make me put that in the vows."

"The vows?" She giggled. "We're already married."

Kai's dark eyes locked on hers as he dropped to his knees before her. "Marry me again. Marry me without a betrothal contract, without an audience. Just you, me, and these vows we have made together."

She shook her head at him. "What would the people of Icelyn think?"

"No one needs to know." He reached for her hand. "But I want to start over. I want to think back to our true wedding day and smile, not cringe."

In truth, she wanted that too. Icelyn could celebrate their public wedding, but that date was not when their marriage began. Soleil mussed his hair with her fingertips. "You'll vow to never ignore me again?" She was half-joking, but Kai did not laugh.

"I will. I was never good at it anyway. You consumed my every waking thought and chased me into my dreams," he told her. "Will you marry me again?"

"I suppose." She sighed. "Although I had gotten used to having that big, decadent bedchamber all to myself."

Kai stood. "I'm afraid that's over, wife." He caught her about the waist and dropped back to the window seat, pulling her into his lap. Soleil blushed. Kai grinned.

No matter, she thought as his lips overtook hers, *I will adjust.*

SOLEIL'S EPILOGUE

Soleil

Northern Nymph Lands

Blaze led the way to the sky scamp, her silver bed in her mouth. The captain called down to Soleil and Kai as they approached. "Oh good! You were running out of time, you know." The old male made a slight bow from his saddle. "No disrespect intended, but the squalls of the Snow Fae Lands wait for no one—not even royalty."

Soleil and Kai exchanged a look. "The squalls have started already?" she asked.

"Just today, princess, according to our guild, but don't worry. They are building from the northeastern coast. We'll get into Icelyn with no trouble if we leave now."

She gave a small, involuntary gasp. Frahst was on the northeast coast. "My twin left for Frahst this morning, at dawn."

"If she left at dawn, she would have made it. If it were, say, mid-morning," he lifted his hand, twisting his wrist and bobbing his head, "she likely would have been diverted to Glacia."

"But you're certain she made it to Frahst if she left at dawn?" she pressed.

"Yes, princess. That much I can say for sure."

"Oh, that's a relief."

The door to the carriage swung open. Blaze needed no further encouragement, hopping inside. She dropped her bed in the corner of one seat. Soleil began to follow when Kai set a hand on her shoulder.

"We should send a message to Wren and Baylee," he said. "They can keep an eye out for Stella among any diverted travelers, just in case. Can you summon a hawk?"

Soleil was certain that Stella had left at dawn but decided it couldn't hurt. She whispered the spell, and the pad of paper, envelope, and pen from her luggage materialized in her hand. The note to her in-laws was hastily written, but she knew they would forgive the informal message, given the situation. Within seconds of her command, a brown and gray feathered courier circled overhead. The hawk dove for the envelope, snatching the letter in its beak, then took off.

Kai helped Soleil into the carriage. She settled in beside Blaze as Kai sat across from them, stretching out his legs. "The imperial guard will have their hands full, with the squalls coming early this year."

She nodded once in agreement. Fortunately, the Snow Fae were skilled in search and rescue during squall season. It was harrowing work, but if any scamps were stranded, they would be found and brought to safety.

"If Stella was diverted, she is welcome to stay with us," he added, "or with Wren and Baylee for a while if the squall prevents her from coming to Icelyn."

"She wasn't diverted. I saw her and Princess Pudge out the door myself, just before sunrise." She gave him a bright smile. "I'm sure Rosette appreciated your offer to stay with us in Icelyn, even though she didn't accept."

He lifted a shoulder. "I knew she wouldn't. She had turned down Phire and Gage as well, but Gage says he will send someone to check on her."

Soleil shook her head to herself. Phire had told her that, but she loved that Kai knew it too—that he cared to know someone was looking out for Rosette and now for Stella. "It's sweet that you're concerned for my sisters."

"Of course, I am." He tugged her into his lap, eliciting a warmth in her cheeks. "It's going in the vows, remember?"

Soleil
Icelyn, Snow Fae Lands

The wind whistled low outside the sky carriage, growing to an ominous howl. Soleil tucked Blaze into the pet bed and held them close to her chest. Kai wrapped his arms around them, shielding them from the biting crystals of ice blasting through the wind as he ushered them outside. The second their feet touched the ground, the sky scamp took off again. Kai saw them into the imperial carriage that waited for them, appointed with hearty dapple-gray horses and a guard in the driver's seat. The horses and the guard were armored from head to toe.

A hawk screeched as Kai took hold of the door handle. The pale gray bird scarcely made it inside, the wind slamming the carriage door closed behind it. A silver envelope stamped with the imperial seal was clenched in its beak. Soleil set Blaze on the seat and tugged the letter from the hawk. Her husband settled in next to her as she read the message out loud.

Kai, Soleil,

We hope this reaches you before the first squall does. Please keep the hawk at your manor; he won't make it back.

Our port authority has confirmed that Stella's scamp was safely diverted here. We shall write again when weather permits.

With love,
Wren and Baylee

"Huh." Soleil dropped her hand to her lap, angling her head at Kai. "I'm positive she left at dawn."

"Well, she is safe in Glacia," he assured her. "We can send for her as soon as there is a break in the squalls."